# THE QUIET AND THE DEAD

## A DCI LUKE WILEY BOOK

### JAYE BAILEY

TWO
YARDS

# Also by Jaye Bailey

**The DCI Luke Wiley Thrillers**

A Grave Return

The Quiet and the Dead

The Killing Pages (coming soon)

# PROLOGUE

After what she had been through over the past six years, the paranoia was always there. She woke every morning in her quiet room and on sunny days the light streamed through the window, the shadows from the tree branches outside dancing on the bedroom walls. She never slept with her curtains drawn, so desperate she still was to feel the light and the air and the outside world around her.

She had created a safe space for herself but she knew she was never safe. She knew they were still out there watching her.

Her three flatmates didn't know anything about her past. They thought they did — she had made up a boring one. She said she had parents and a sister and they lived up north. One weekend when her flatmates were all away, she took the opportunity to lie and say that she too would be away, visiting her family. Instead, she stayed in the flat, enjoying the peace and quiet and above all, she enjoyed the space. She couldn't have visited her family anyway, even though she was desperate to see them.

She knew that she could not be complacent. She could not

give into temptation. She could not do so many things that she wanted to do.

But everyone has a weakness.

————

Her weakness was her father. She had missed him more than anyone else over the past six years. It was like an ache in her chest that sometimes made it difficult to breathe. What would he have been thinking all of this time? How did he manage without her? Did he know she didn't mean for this to happen?

The two of them had been as close as a father and daughter could be and when she saw him by complete accident the previous week on a busy London street, she had stopped dead in her tracks. She never ventured to her old neighbourhood and had purposely moved to the opposite side of the city. Her father shouldn't have been there. This chance encounter shouldn't have happened.

And her father shouldn't have been in a wheelchair.

She couldn't believe it. She wanted to rush to him, to throw her arms around her father. What had happened? Why was he being pushed down the street by someone she didn't recognize?

The urge to see him again was too great. She needed to be close to him, even if she could not let him see her. It was the only thing she could do.

This is how she found herself outside her old house, the house she had not seen in six years. She loitered about half a block away, pretending to look at her phone, occasionally walking past her old front door and then turning around and walking past it again. She couldn't see anything and her father did not appear. But she knew that her family was still living there. The garden gnome she had picked out seven years earlier at the local garden centre — ridiculed by everyone in her family except her father — was in its usual spot to the right of the front door.

She had been warned not to go back. She had been told of the severe consequences. But what is stronger — fear or love?

Three days later her body was found floating in the canal. She had been warned.

# ONE

Detective Chief Inspector Luke Wiley couldn't sleep. It wasn't a crushing insomnia but rather a sense of dread that kept him awake and wouldn't go away. He wasn't used to not being able to fall asleep. Even with the toughest cases, even when his mind was spinning endlessly he used to be able to float off into unconsciousness within minutes of his head hitting the pillow. It used to drive his wife nuts.

Sadie would usually be in bed before him, cocooned into the duvet and a book from the teetering stack on her bedside table propped up on his pillow while she turned the pages, completely engrossed. She loved to get into bed early and considered the bed a sort of refuge of comfort and quiet time to herself. She liked an excellent thread count and sheets that were partly made from bamboo. She chose soft glow light-bulbs in the bedroom and used a different fabric softener in the laundry for the flannel long sleeved shirts she wore to bed through most of the year.

Luke used to marvel at it all as he was the kind of person

who just fell into bed in a t-shirt and was asleep within minutes. The ritual and the details of Sadie's bedtime routine wasn't something he ever could have imagined for himself. Except the high thread count sheets. The introduction of this softness into his life was incredible. Sadie had been incredible. And now she was gone.

Funnily enough, Luke had no trouble sleeping in the weeks after Sadie died. Everyone had asked how he was sleeping — it seemed to be a safe question for all of the people in his life who didn't know what else to say to him.

How do you convey your deepest sympathy and concern for someone who is going through the worst time in their life while simultaneously being frightened of the depth of their grief? Luke understood that it was difficult and he felt himself feeling sorry for his friends, feeling sorry for his colleagues who didn't know how to help him. He didn't know how to help himself.

But Luke did fall asleep with ease at the end of each of these wretched days. He supposed it was partly wanting to be in a space that his wife loved so much. He could still smell her on the sheets, her stack of books was still on the bedside table, her lip balm next to it. It was also because he felt an exhaustion he had never felt before. His grief was breathtaking and by the end of the day, Luke simply had nothing left within himself. He felt completely depleted and so he slept.

But now Luke would do anything to have those first days and weeks of shock and grief back because what he was dealing with was so much worse. He still longed for his wife in a desperate, aching way but now he had the knowledge that he had failed her.

Sadie's death was not an accident. It was not a cruel twist of fate that her car skidded off a slippery road as she swerved to avoid an animal. It was not bad luck that this happened next to a lake and her car submerged too quickly for her to escape. Her death had been calculated and deliberate and her killer walked away into the shadows, never to be seen again.

But Luke would find him.

# Two

I n the two months since Luke had come back to work, his partner had been simultaneously thrilled and incredibly bored.

Detective Sergeant Hana Sawatsky hated being bored.

She sat at her desk in the Serious Crimes Unit on the seventh floor of New Scotland Yard and thumbed through the mountain of paperwork their current case was generating. Not all police work was going to have a detective on the edge of their seat and not all crimes were created equal, but as cases went, the one they were working on had to be one of the most boring of both of their careers.

A man was harassing various people in his neighbourhood, these people had all had quite enough of it, and decided to file complaints and requests for a restraining order in the same fortnight. Two dozen accusations of stalking had to be dealt with — all of the neighbours interviewed individually, all recorded, all investigated and the paperwork that went with this was immense.

Why was Detective Chief Inspector Luke Wiley the person assigned to a case like this, several hundred times less important than his rank? The answer was quite simple. His superior officer, Chief Inspector Stephen O'Donnell couldn't stand his guts. And Hana Sawatsky, as Luke's partner on the force, was along for the ride. A really boring, tedious ride.

The day hadn't been going particularly well. As Luke and Hana had sat through yet more hours of seemingly endless administration, Luke had finally lost it. Slamming his coffee down on the desk so the coffee splashed up and out of the mug and across his desk, the expletives that were heard by Hana, whose desk was just outside of Luke's office at least made her smile. Her partner wasn't one for swearing for the sake of it. He meant that expletive and she knew exactly who it was meant for.

Stephen O'Donnell was a prick at the best of times but when Luke Wiley was suddenly back at work on the Serious Crimes Unit and back in his old office as if he had never left, O'Donnell seemed to now be on a mission to make Luke's life as miserable as possible.

It was, Hana had to admit, working.

Luke appeared at the door of his office and shook his head at Hana.

'Don't do it,' Hana said.

Luke didn't respond except to continue shaking his head as he stormed down the hall towards O'Donnell's glass fronted office at the end of the unit. Luke didn't ask to be invited inside.

'This is absolutely ridiculous, Stephen. You are wasting police resources having Sawatsky and me on this nonsense case. You know it and I know it.'

O'Donnell leaned back in his chair, which Hana knew would only infuriate Luke further. Their Chief Inspector never seemed to be doing any work himself. There was a lot of sitting around and leaning back in chairs.

'DCI Wiley, are you not taking this case seriously?'

'Jesus, Stephen. Are you kidding me?'

'I most certainly am not. Here we have a potentially extremely dangerous stalker and over two dozen victims. Their lives are at risk and this is considered a high risk case. Any mistake here — and you do tend to make them, Wiley — would be a critical failure.'

'These people are not in danger, Stephen. They are curtain twitching busybodies and your stalker is a run of the mill jerk who has a lot of time on his hands. I've spoken to every single one of them and the only person who is in danger is you if you lean any further back in that chair.'

O'Donnell snapped upright and glared at Luke.

'I'd strongly suggest that you take this case seriously.'

'We are Serious Crime,' Luke said. 'This is not serious and I'm struggling to see that any crime has yet been committed. How did this even get up to the seventh floor of Scotland Yard?'

At this question, O'Donnell began to smile and Luke knew he had been played. This case wasn't in the remit of the Serious Crime Unit and everyone knew it. O'Donnell had plucked this from some other department — he'd probably had a couple of his guys on the lower floors on the lookout for something tedious, something that he knew would infuriate Detective Chief Inspector Luke Wiley. And there was absolutely nothing he could do about it.

*What a goddamn waste of time*, Luke thought to himself as he stood there in O'Donnell's office having this futile conversation. Luke opened his mouth to say what he really wanted to say but then thought better of it and instead cleared his throat.

'Nothing else then, I take it?' asked O'Donnell.

'No, Sir.'

'Shut the door on your way out.'

Luke closed the door behind him just a little too loudly

and Hana involuntarily winced as she watched Luke walk down the hallway back towards her.

'Lunch?' he said, not stopping at her desk but continuing to stride towards the lift.

Hana closed the file folder in front of her, grabbed her jacket and followed her partner down the hall. They were silent in the lift but Hana was quite desperate to say something.

'Not now, Hana,' Luke said.

She couldn't help but chuckle.

'And you're buying lunch,' he continued.

The lift doors opened and the two detectives stepped outside and walked towards the back entrance of Scotland Yard where they would turn right and head towards their favourite little bistro next to King's College.

'Oh I don't think so, Wiley. It's your fault my life has become a complete and utter bore. This one's on you.'

When they had been seated at their usual table and had ordered their usual meals — club sandwich for Luke and roast chicken and chips for Hana — Luke apologized for the situation they found themselves in.

'It's not your fault, Luke. The guy hates you, he thought he had gotten rid of you forever when you left the force and in no way did he ever think you would come back to work.'

'There was always the possibility that I was going to come back to work though.'

At this comment, Hana put down her knife and fork, finished her mouthful of chips and said, 'Not really, dude.'

'Sure there was.'

'Okay, sure there was. Objectively. But your wife died and you inherited all of her money. You don't need to work. That's also why O'Donnell hates you. If he had your kind of money, we'd never see him again.'

'Think I should give it to him?'

Hana chortled. 'If the rest of this year is like it is now, I'll insist on it.'

'I really am sorry, Hana. You could request to be reassigned to a different detective. It's not the end of the world if we aren't partners.'

'It isn't? I thought you couldn't function without me.'

Now it was Luke's turn to laugh. Except there was an element of truth to what Hana had just said. He wondered if she knew this, too.

For the past two months since Luke had discovered that his wife's death was not an accident, he and Hana had been spending most of their waking hours outside of the tedium being thrown at them by their superior officer slowly piecing through Luke's old cases to see if there was any kind of clue.

'I could come over this evening and we could lay out what we both have and see if there are any threads we can pick up,' Hana offered.

'Thanks, Hana. I have Nicky this evening, but why don't you come over in the morning if you're up?'

'Oh I'll be up.'

Luke waited for Hana to say the one thing she had been saying for the past two months.

'You need to tell her, Luke.'

'I really understand why you are saying this, but not right now. It's just too soon. I don't know what we are dealing with yet.'

Hana didn't like this response. It made the hairs on the back of her neck stand up and if the past was anything to go by, this was a really bad sign.

# THREE

Luke, of course, understood why Hana wanted him to tell his therapist that Sadie's death was not an accident. She was worried about him and who could blame her?

But nothing was more important, more critical, to him than finding out who had killed his wife. He couldn't bring her back and all of the nights he paced his house wishing that he could and all of the mornings he woke wondering how he could go on without her now finally felt like they had a purpose. He would find this son of a bitch.

Luke knew that Hana felt the same way. She had loved Sadie deeply and wanted to catch her killer. But Sadie also didn't know his therapist. She didn't sit in the room with her and understand what that process was like for him. She also hadn't really thought it through.

What exactly was Luke supposed to say to Nicky?

Was he supposed to say to her one session, *Look here's a bit of a strange one. I received some anonymous photographs that showed my wife had been kidnapped and forced off the road while she was driving and the guy stood next to her car while she drowned.*

Luke trusted his therapist implicitly but he was going to guess that this kind of information fell into the remit of breaking confidentiality. A crime had been committed and a suspect was still at large and there was the possibility that if someone had murdered his wife, then Luke was in danger as well and Nicky may also feel the authorities should be told. It had only been a couple of months since he turned up at Nicky's front door, his arm in a sling with a broken collarbone, and looking a little more than worse for wear. She had been alarmed and Luke wasn't sure that any more information about the darker side of his life at the moment was going to be helpful.

His dead wife made his life dark enough already.

The wind had whipped up as Luke walked the forty minutes from his house to Nicky's and it was that dreary time of year when the leaves were falling from the trees in bunches, becoming wet and slippery underfoot as they waited to be swept away. The pavement had felt like a ice rink of foliage on the walk, but Luke was relieved to get some fresh air after a day of paperwork in his office.

Luke knew that he must be the last session of Nicky's day at seven o'clock in the evening and he wondered what she would do after he left. Sometimes when he arrived at this time there would be a pot of something delicious simmering on the stove that he could just see out of the corner of his eye as he walked past the entrance to the kitchen and headed upstairs to her office.

Luke was sure that Nicky lived here alone. Occasionally there were shoes by the inside of the door tugged off on a wet day and left to dry, and there was always just one pair that would fit his therapist. Once the door to the bathroom was left open and Luke noticed a lone toothbrush sitting in a cup by the sink.

On a cold evening like today, if there was supper waiting on her stove, Luke found himself yearning to stay after his session was over. To sit with this woman he barely knew and open a bottle of wine and sit across from her at the inviting dining room table he walked by every time he entered the house and continue talking into the night.

It was an odd sensation for Luke, to know almost nothing about Dr. Nicky Bowman and yet she knew lots of intimate details about him. The role reversal from his usual situation — the blank slate detective learning everything about his suspect, the victim; and often in ways that were surprising — it was so striking to him. He found himself often feeling desperate to know more about his therapist. Who exactly was this woman that he found himself trusting, against every fibre of his personality, with his grief and his fear and his deep love for the wife he had lost?

And how insensitive of him to assume that she did not have someone about to arrive the moment he walked out the door and closed it behind him. That there wasn't a partner, a friend, someone to share what smelled tonight like coq au vin, steaming away in the kitchen.

It would just be Luke at home alone later tonight, probably having poached eggs on rye toast and a large glass of wine, sitting at his kitchen table surrounded by files he had duplicated from the office so they wouldn't be discovered missing, and a laptop that never left the tabletop because he was on it continuously the moment he got home. There weren't any dinner parties being hosted around that table anymore.

Luke knocked on the door and it opened almost immediately, as if Nicky had been waiting for him just the other side of it.

'Hi, Luke.'

'Hi,' he said, and ducked into the house.

He followed her up the stairs as usual and thought about what Hana had said to him at lunch. Would he feel better if he divulged to Nicky that they thought Sadie had been murdered? The answer was pretty clear: not one bit.

When they were seated, Nicky jumped straight in.

'One bit of housekeeping before we start, if you don't mind?'

'Oh, sure.'

'I've had an email from the EAP at your work?'

'Yes,' Luke replied. 'That's the Employee Assistance Program. They are the ones technically looking after my mental health as I returned to work. I'm sorry about this — was it a form that you needed to fill out to assure them that I'm not crazy?'

'Something like that,' Nicky said. 'It's no problem — mostly box ticking. It's just that the email was cc'd to someone. Marina Scott-Carson. I googled her and, well, correct me if I'm wrong but it looks like she's as senior as it gets at the Met.'

'Yes, she's my boss.'

'I thought your boss was called Stephen and you hated him.'

Luke couldn't help but laugh.

'Yes, that's correct. Marina is my boss's boss, so also my boss.'

'Are you surprised that she was copied on this email?'

Luke leant forward on the couch, slightly puzzled by this line of questioning.

'Not necessarily. She was the one who pulled the strings to get me back, and to make sure that I was partnered with Hana again. Why are you asking?'

Nicky paused. Luke sat up straighter as the one thing Nicky never did was hesitate before she spoke.

'What is it?'

'She left me a voice mail. I didn't pick up the call because I was with another patient, but she has asked me to call her back. And she gave me her mobile phone number, specifically asking me to call her back on it and not at Scotland Yard.'

Luke took in this information and could almost feel it flipping over in his mind as he considered what it meant.

'I'm sorry about this, Nicky. I think the circumstances surrounding my return to work weren't ideal and she needs reassurance that I'm functioning okay. I mean, that I'm not a crying mess on your couch who is likely to screw up whatever case I'm working on.'

'And do you feel you are handling what you're working on now competently?'

'Oh,' Luke said. 'Pretty sure.'

Now it was Nicky's turn to take in what he was saying. She pursed her lips and nodded at Luke, as if to say that she would leave it there and give him top marks when she eventually called Marina Scott-Carson back.

'How do you feel everything is going for you?' Nicky asked.

'Well, I'm not really sleeping very well at the moment.'

'Oh I don't trust people who sleep well. Hugely suspect.'

Luke smiled at his therapist and breathed a small sigh of relief. His thoughts exactly.

# Four

It wasn't yet seven o'clock in the morning and Luke and Hana were already on their second cafetière of coffee, both of them with their legs stretched out onto the chairs around Luke's kitchen table.

They hadn't looked at the photographs that had been anonymously posted through Luke's front door in some time. Right after they had turned up, they both looked at them obsessively. It had been one of the worst moments of both of their lives, perhaps only second to the news that Sadie had died. As they gripped onto each other, both sitting on the floor of the kitchen they sat in again this morning, Hana had initially told Luke to put the photos down and not touch them again. But they realized very quickly that there would be no DNA analysis of these images. Whoever had delivered them would be the same person who had left the warning note days before and the analysis on that came up empty.

The detectives also knew that whoever had done this might be quite close to them. They had discussed bringing on board the one person they both trusted over anyone else at the Met — Laura Rowdy. If you had asked either Luke or Hana what Laura's official job title was, they wouldn't have a clue. But Rowdy was indispensable. She was the ultimate fixer and knew absolutely everyone. If you needed evidence analyzed, if you needed surveillance footage, if you needed to track someone down who had seemingly disappeared she could do it. But Rowdy also needed assistance to obtain this kind of information and the Met's systems could sometimes store data that they were not supposed to store. Even if they trusted Rowdy, could they trust those around her?

The photographs themselves were not of the greatest quality. They had either been printed at home with a good printer and photographic paper, or they had been printed from a kiosk at a chemist or printing shop. Could they request to see every stored image at every kiosk in the country and filter them until they found a possible location where the photos had been printed, leading them to CCTV coverage? It was needle in a haystack territory and so all of a sudden the hunt for Sadie's killer became an old school investigation. And Luke and Hana didn't mind in the slightest.

Hana yawned and poured more milk into her already milky coffee, then stood up to go and put her mug in the microwave.

'At least I feel like I'm doing something useful here,' she said.

'The worst part is that it's Friday and I'm sure that somehow O'Donnell is going to concoct some other bullshit complaint that is going to take up our entire weekend. I'm really sorry if that's the case, Hana.'

Hana waved her hand and gingerly took her mug, now too hot to touch, out of the microwave.

'Do you have plans this weekend?'

She hesitated slightly before answering that she did not, and wondered if Luke picked up on it. She loved her partner dearly, as she had loved his wife, but the past few months of

Luke being brought back to the Met by an old case, and then deciding to come back to work full-time, and then trying to piece together what had happened to Sadie, had begun to take a little bit of a toll. She wasn't overwhelmed, or even particularly tired, but she felt a yearning to do something more for herself. She also knew that the second she told Luke what her plans were this weekend, he would want to know all about it and then once more, it wouldn't be just hers.

Sitting back down at the kitchen table, Hana's mobile phone began to buzz. She looked at the screen and then turned the phone to face Luke.

It was Stephen O'Donnell calling.

'Oh christ,' Hana said. 'I am not answering it. You're right, he's trying to take the weekend and I'm not having it. It's seven o'clock in the morning. I'm still in bed. I'm in the shower. I don't care where I am but I'm not taking this call.'

The phone stopped and they both stared at it, waiting for one final buzz to tell them that he had left a voice mail.

They both jumped slightly as instead, it was Luke's phone that sprung to life.

It was Stephen O'Donnell.

'Don't you dare, Luke.'

Luke began to laugh out loud.

'Hana. I will deal with the weekend work. Don't worry.'

Luke picked up the phone and swiped right to answer.

'Good morning, Stephen. To what do I owe the pleasure of this early morning call?'

Luke's face suddenly fell and Hana understood immediately that this was not the sort of call she thought it would be.

Luke placed the phone down on the table and hit the speaker button.

'I'm sorry, Commander. Could you please repeat that?'

Hana stood very still, not able to remember the last time that Luke addressed their boss by his rank.

'A young woman's body has been found. She was in the water in the canal just off Broadway Market. Officers are there but I need you and Sawatsky at the scene.'

'You want us, Sir?'

There was a pause on the line.

'There's no time to relish the moment, Wiley. Hackett and Smith are deep into their investigation and I'm not pulling them off it. There's no one else from our unit available.'

'Understood, Sir.'

'Rowdy will send you the coordinates and Sawatsky isn't answering her phone, so I'll need you to wake her up.'

Hana bit her lip and tried not to make a sound.

'Thank you, Sir.'

Luke pressed his phone to hang up the call and Hana was already clearing their mugs of coffee away. So much for her weekend plans.

'Awake, Hana?'

'I'm driving.'

# FIVE

I t had begun to rain when Hana and Luke pulled up at the closest pedestrian entrance to the canal in the east end of London. It was the kind of rain that drizzled and an umbrella would be useless. Both the detectives pulled up the hoods of their jackets as they walked through the metal barriers that were there to prevent cyclists from speeding from the road down to the canal walkway and walked towards the scrum of police officers at the side of the water.

One of them strode towards Luke and introduced himself.

'Sir, I'm Constable Parker.'

'Were you first on the scene, Constable?'

'Yes, Sir. My partner and I were here within a couple of minutes of the call. We secured the area and the man who called emergency services is waiting to be spoken to over there. The medical examiner has arrived and we are ready to assist in pulling her out if required, Sir.'

'Alright. Let's have a look, shall we?'

Hana and Luke were accompanied over to the water's edge by Officer Parker and Luke asked for his torch. Shining the light into the water, they could see a woman floating face down. Her body was gently moving in the still waters of the canal, and she had become wedged between the back of a houseboat and the cement wall that rose a few feet up to where they were standing.

Luke looked around to see if anyone was wearing water-proof gear but only saw Dr. Chung, the medical examiner shielding her phone from the rain next to the van that would take the body away.

'I'm happy to go in, Sir,' said Parker.

'Let's wait another ten minutes or so. I'd like forensics to take some photographs when it's finally light. We're almost there,' Luke said, looking up at the sky.

Hana was walking alongside one of the houseboats that was sheltering the woman's body from the rest of the open canal.

'I assume you've already knocked?' she asked.

'Yes, Ma'am. Doesn't appear to be anyone living there at present.'

The boat looked like it hadn't been inhabited for some time. It certainly hadn't been moved. Moss was growing over the sides of the boat, the ropes were covered in algae and the windows were opaque with grime that was probably on both sides of the glass.

'We're going to need to get in here anyway,' Luke said.

'You might have an easier time with the other boat, Sir,' said Parker.

'Really? It looks the same to me. Like it hasn't been moved or lived in for awhile.'

'Maybe, Sir. But if you walk down a bit and hold your hand close to the metal pipe just there. Careful not to touch it.'

Luke followed the young officer's instructions and as he

brought his hand towards the pipe, he could immediately feel the warmth emanating from it. Someone inside had been burning their wood stove a few hours earlier.

'Excellent, Parker. Is there anyone inside?'

'No response to knocking, Sir. And I was quite clear that it was the police knocking. Might have sworn, Sir.'

If Hana had been standing closer to Parker, she imagine she would have seen him wink when he said this.

'Well, let's try again shall we?' she said as she walked over to where the door was located, hopped onto the frame of the boat and lifted her leg. Both Parker and Luke involuntarily winced as Hana brought her boot down into the door as she shouted.

'Police. Wakey, wakey!'

With the third kick, the door of the boat gave way with a mighty crack and Hana ricocheted back slightly, into the waiting arms of Officer Parker.

'Well done, Ma'am.'

Luke looked over at the two of them, rolled his eyes and ducked his head into the boat. It was almost pitch black inside and stank of cigarette smoke. Blinds were pulled down everywhere and the only crack of light coming in was from a broken blind towards the stern of the boat. Still holding Parker's torch, Luke switched it on and scanned the inside of the boat. The beam of light picked up movement halfway inside and Luke stopped his torch to focus on it.

An arm suddenly appeared from underneath a raft of wool blankets and Luke moved quickly to jump down inside the entrance to the boat.

'Police. Stand up, please.'

The figure was barely moving but with an arm up in front of the figure's face, trying to shield from the bright light that Luke was pointing at it.

'Are you injured?' Luke said.

'Jesus,' the figure mumbled, 'What's going on?'

Luke stepped a little closer and shone the light directly at the figure's face. It was a man, probably in his mid-thirties and clearly extremely hungover. Two empty vodka bottles were tipped over on their side on the floor next to him and Luke could suddenly smell the unmistakable scent of old vomit.

'What's your name?'

'Why do you want to know?'

Luke was not in the mood for for this kind of bullshit and taking a page from Hana's morning grumpiness, took two big steps over to the man, hauled him to his feet and pushed him towards the door. Parker and Hana finished the exercise by pulling him outside and had him on the ground in a hold, checking for weapons and any drugs or other paraphernalia, and then pulled him back into a sitting position on the pavement.

It was finally light outside and the man squinted at them, then coughed and spat in Luke's direction.

'One more time. What is your name?' Luke said.

'It's Robert. Robert Briggs.'

'Do you live here?'

'Sort of.'

'What does that mean?' Hana asked.

'It means I sort of live here.'

'Do you know that there is a dead woman floating next to where you sort of live?' Luke said.

'Nothing to do with me,' Briggs answered.

'I bet it fucking does,' Parker whispered audibly.

'How are forensics doing with the body?' Luke asked.

Hana stepped aside to speak to them and Parker swayed back and forth on his feet, as if he wanted to pick Briggs up and throw him with one arm into the canal. Luke smiled to himself as he remembered the feeling well. He still got it from time to time, that immediate rush of anger, that sense that you knew someone had done something really bad and needed to held to account, even if you weren't quite sure exactly what it was yet. But mostly, with experience, came the knowledge that you had to sit with what was in front of you to make sure that you got it right and that every angle had been covered. It was a difficult skill to acquire, and many officers never got there. His boss was one of them. But in Parker he saw a bit of himself as a younger man — sightly too eager, slightly too self-righteous, but someone who would do anything that would help that young woman in the water, whatever had happened to her — and he put his hand on young officer's shoulder.

Luke could see Hana walking back towards him with the forensic officers, their cameras covered in waterproof pouches and Dr. Chung was approaching him from the van. It was time to bring the woman out of the water.

'Parker, would you be so kind as to lift Mr. Briggs up so I can speak to him properly?'

'Sir,' Parker replied and effortlessly hoisted Briggs up to a standing position, one of his hands holding him up in what would have been a painful spot just under his ribs.

Briggs grunted and spat again.

'Who lives on this boat?'

'It's my mate's. He's away. I'm staying for a bit.'

Luke was unsure how much information he was going to get out of Briggs, who was clearly still drunk.

'Where were you last night?'

'Here. On the boat.'

'Were you here all night?'

'Yes.'

'Were you alone?'

'Yes.'

'Did you see anyone else along the canal last night?'

'No one comes down here.'

'Not really what I asked, Mr. Briggs. Did you see anyone on the canal at any point last night?'

Briggs shuffled and Parker jabbed his hand a little more firmly under his ribs.

'No,' Briggs wheezed. 'I ain't seen no one. No one.'

'Maybe a ride down to the station for Mr. Briggs. What do you think, Parker?'

'I think it's a good idea, Sir.'

Parker led Briggs over to one of the police cars parked at the top of the canal entrance and handed him to two other officers. The forensic officers spoke to Luke and confirmed they had taken all of the photos they needed before heading into Brigg's houseboat to repeat the process there.

Dr. Chung walked towards Luke and handed him a cup of coffee.

'Thank you, Chung. Where did you get this in this part of town so early in the morning?'

'I didn't. One of the forensic guys offered it to me. Thought you might need it more.'

What Luke really felt he needed after handling Briggs was to wash his hands. He wiped one of them on his trousers and Chung pulled out a small bottle of hand sanitizer.

'You're a genius, Chung,' Luke said as he put his coffee down on the ground and squirted some of the gel into his palms, rubbing them together.

Coffee back in hand, the two of them walked towards the canal where Parker was waiting with the other three officers he had assembled to go into the water.

'Right,' Luke said. 'Very gently, please.'

The four officers eased themselves into the canal, all of them wincing and breathing heavily as they entered the water which must have been freezing at this time of year. The water was just over all of their waists and they carefully maneuvered to surround the body before slowly lifting her up and towards the other two officers waiting with Hana, Luke and Dr. Chung.

Luke had been so focused on the scene that he hadn't registered the significance of what was happening. But Dr. Chung and Hana clearly had.

The two women stood on either side of him, as if to shield him from the thought of how this would have happened to Sadie as well when she was pulled out of her submerged car and out of the lake.

'Do you want to step aside and let them work for a second?' Hana whispered to him.

Luke said nothing and shook his head.

'How's the coffee, Wiley?' Chung asked.

He turned to her and tried to look reassuring.

'I'm fine, Chung.'

The woman's body was pulled out and placed onto her back on the waiting gurney. They could finally see her face.

'Oh no,' Hana said, quietly.

It was what they were all thinking.

The woman was very young, late teens or barely into adulthood. Her hair was probably quite a light blonde, although it was hard to tell when it was wet. She was white, her lips a dark purple and her eyes were open, the pupils dark, the blood vessels in both eyeballs having ruptured.

She was in jeans that were suctioned tightly to her legs and the green puffer jacket she was wearing was beginning to lose its shape from being in the water for many hours.

'The jacket is probably what kept her afloat to get stuck here,' Hana said. 'Air pockets in the lining.'

'Yes,' mused Luke. She couldn't have travelled far in this water. There's barely any current. It's possible she fell in here. Maybe she was walking in the dark and lost her footing. There aren't any streetlamps. It was hard to see when we arrived, even with the police lights.'

'I don't think so, Wiley,' said Dr. Chung as she hovered over the young woman's body. Very gently, Dr. Chung put her gloved hand on the girl's forehead and delicately swept back a piece of wet hair that was stuck across one of her eyes. Parker shifted uncomfortably on his feet, watching such a heartbreaking gesture, as if Dr. Chung was allowing the dead girl to be able to see again.

'Here, and here,' she pointed at the body, and Luke and Hana peered in for a closer look.

'Ligature marks around her neck — you can see the bruising already starting to bloom. And the blood vessels in the eyes. She was most likely strangled. When I get her back to the lab, I doubt I'll find any water in her lungs. She was probably dead before she went in.'

'So homicide,' Luke said.

'You know I don't like to be definitive before we get a body back to where I can take a proper look, but almost certainly. I'm sorry, Luke.'

He nodded and pulled out his mobile.

'One more thing,' Dr. Chung said. 'She hasn't been in the water all that long. Less than eight hours, I'd say, just by looking at her. I'll do an internal body temp when I get back, but...'

'The quicker we move, the quicker we'll get him,' Luke said.

Luke pressed a couple of buttons on his phone and waited for it to ring. When O'Donnell picked up, Luke filled him in on what they had in front of them, and that it didn't look good.

'We'll need divers, Stephen.'

'Sending now. Any ID yet?'

'Working on it.'

Any bag that the girl was carrying was probably at the bottom of the canal and Hana delicately searched her pockets, first the puffer jacket and then very carefully, her skintight jeans. There was nothing to be found.

'Okay,' said Luke. 'Let's get her back and then take it from there. Rowdy can run some image scans from photographs that forensics will have by now.'

'Do you want to speak to the man who called it in?' Parker asked.

'Sure, the poor guy probably would like to get home. I'll go over to him now. You've done a great job, Parker. Go and get yourself some breakfast.'

'I'd rather stay and continue to search the scene, Sir.'

Luke smiled at him.

'Be my guest.'

As Hana and Luke began to trudge their way back up to street level where their car was parked, Parker suddenly shouted for them.

'Detectives, I think you need to see this.'

Hana and Luke and Dr. Chung walked back to the body of the girl, lifeless and staring at the sky. Parker pointed to her right boot, still snug around the girl's foot. Poking out, lodged between her sock and the inside of her boot was something plastic and orange.

'Gloves, Luke,' said Hana.

Luke pulled an unused pair of gloves out of his jacket pocket and handed them to her. She snapped them on and delicately tugged at the piece of plastic.

'I can't quite get it.'

'Here,' Parker said, gently holding and twisting the girl's boot to the left so that Hana could get a better grip with her fingers, now slippery with the water still dripping off the girl. Slowly, Hana pulled upwards and a small plastic rectangle appeared. Hana held it up.

'It's a debit card. From National Trust Bank. I have the same one,' Parker said.

Hana peered at the card.

'Emma Jones,' she said softly. 'This is Emma Jones.'

'Well, Emma,' said Luke. 'Why were you keeping your bank card inside your boot?'

# SIX

Hana had asked Parker to get in the back of the car and drive with them to Scotland Yard for one primary reason — food. She was absolutely starving and knew that Luke wouldn't be stopping to do anything except find the person who killed Emma Jones for the rest of the day.

'Thank you for bringing me along,' Parker said from the back seat as Hana sped down the Embankment, dodging as much traffic as she could by slipping in and out of the bus lane.

'You could just put the light on and go,' Luke said.

'This is more fun. Parker, you might want to write this down. I like my bagel toasted lightly, with egg and ham. Plain if they have it, sesame seed if they don't. On both sides of the bagel I like ketchup and don't be shy with it. Large latte with only one shot of espresso. And a Diet Coke.'

'Jesus,' said Luke.

'What can I get for you, Sir?'

'Any bagel, bit of cream cheese. Large black coffee. Thank you.'

'I'll be on it as soon as we get there.'

Luke could see Parker leaning to his left slightly to get a better look at Hana while she was driving. He tried not to let Parker see that he had noticed, and he also tried not to chuckle.

'What?' Hana asked.

'Nothing,' Luke shrugged and pulled out his phone.

'I doubt that Rowdy will be in yet, but I'm going to try her,' Luke said, picking up the evidence bag in his lap that held the bank card and staring at it. The phone rang only once before Rowdy picked up.

'What do you need, Luke? I'm here. I heard on the radio that a body had been found in the canal off Victoria Park and that you and Hana had been sent over. Is it bad?'

'Do you keep a police radio on at home, next to your bed?' Luke asked.

'None of your business, Detective Chief Inspector.'

Luke laughed aloud and knew that this moment of levity was the only one they were going to have today. He had missed teasing Laura Rowdy and he knew that she had probably missed it more.

'I'm sorry, Rowdy, but yes it's not good. We have pulled out a young woman and the only thing she had on her was a bank card. Ready?'

Luke read her the details as Hana sped past Waterloo Bridge, the stream of pedestrians walking across it from the train station towards the Strand like a steady current of water that crossed the opposite flow of the Thames below it. Umbrellas were still up and the day didn't seem to be brightening at all. Soon Christmas lights would begin popping up across the city, but there were still a few weeks left of the dreary days between the clocks slipping an hour backwards and the festive spirit of the approaching holiday.

'This has the potential to get big very quickly,' Hana said.

'I know,' Luke replied. 'Today is important. We will work as efficiently as we can.'

'What do you mean by this getting big very quickly?' Parker asked from the back seat.

Luke swiveled around as much as he could to look at their new companion.

'With a situation like this — a young girl murdered in the middle of London — news will spread very quickly. There's an element of fear with this kind of killing and an element of voyeurism that can be unpleasant. The second the journalists have it, we lose time.'

'How is that?' Parker asked.

'Too much time dealing with press and not enough time catching a killer,' Hana replied, pulling into the back entrance of Scotland Yard. 'The bagel place is that way.'

While Parker headed off to get breakfast, the detectives entered Scotland Yard and headed up to the seventh floor. Stepping out of the lift, they could feel that the atmosphere in the unit had changed since yesterday. The air felt charged with everyone's sense of urgency heightened and it was very quiet.

Luke and Hana walked down the hall towards the Incident Room and as they suspected, it had been set up already. The white board that covered the entire back wall had been cleaned and set up with fresh unused pens and two dozen magnets along its side, waiting to be of use. Luke hated the sight of a blank board. It was too full of possibilities, too empty of direction. A full board meant they were closer to solving the crime and they wanted to get there as quickly as possible today.

O'Donnell emerged from his office at the end of the hall and put his suit jacket on. Even he meant business this morning and everyone began to file into the room.

'Right,' O'Donnell said. 'The divers are en route to the scene and will be scouring for evidence for 2 miles in both directions of where the body was found. Dr. Chung is already performing the autopsy in her lab and we'll have the preliminary report later today. Never easy to get good DNA from a body that's been pulled out of the water, but we'll hopefully get something. Detective Chief Inspector?'

Luke stood up and walked towards the blank white board. He picked up a pen and wrote in big, bold letters at the top: EMMA JONES

'The body we found in the canal this morning had no ID on her except for a debit bank card. The bank card belongs to an Emma Jones. Until we have a positive ID, we don't know if this girl is, indeed, Emma Jones but we will be able to confirm it this morning. She was found in the canal just below Broadway Market in Hackney by a man walking his dog. She was found around a quarter past six and it was pitch dark down there. The only reason she was seen was because the dog was sniffing at the water's edge and the man was wearing a headlamp. When I questioned him earlier, he said he didn't see anyone for the twenty minutes or so that he had been walking down there as it's a quiet part of the canal. Not a lot to go on. But we're lucky to have a bit of a head start before this breaks.'

Luke put the pen down and took a moment to look at every face in the room.

'I'd like to be very clear about something. This young woman has been murdered. We are going to have to tell her family. I want this locked down. No speaking to the press. No leaks.'

'Wiley, we will have to involve the press here,' O'Donnell interrupted.

'Not yet.'

'You know it's inevitable, Wiley. We'll brief them ASAP.'

'We will absolutely not, Sir.'

The two men stared at each other, the only two people

standing in the room. O'Donnell grimaced and puffed out his chest.

'I will dictate how we run this. No one else and furthermore...'

The door to the Incident Room flew open and Officer Parker stumbled inside, his hands full of large cardboard cups of coffee, bags of bagels and a Diet Coke.

'Sorry, they said you were down here,' he offered apologetically.

'Who the hell are you?' snapped O'Donnell.

Parker's mouth opened but no sound came out — the young man suddenly aware of his rank and where found he was standing in this room on the seventh floor of Scotland Yard in a morning of events he had not anticipated.

'Commander O'Donnell, may I introduce Officer Parker of Division...?'

'Twenty two, Sir,' Parker stammered.

'Officer Parker of Division twenty two. Heroic efforts with the victim this morning. Absolutely essential to the case. He's with me and Sawatsky,' Luke said.

Parker smiled at O'Donnell.

'I'm sorry, Sir. I would have taken your breakfast order if I'd known.'

'Don't worry about that, Parker,' Luke said. 'He's a robot, doesn't eat food.'

Before O'Donnell had time to explode, Laura Rowdy appeared at the door.

'I have an address for Emma Jones.'

# SEVEN

'What do we have apart from an address?' Luke asked Rowdy after the rest of the room had dispersed.

'Nothing, I'm afraid,' she replied. 'Banks aren't exactly forthcoming without cause, even to the police. Privacy issues. I'll have more for you in a couple of hours, but thought you'd want to start with this.'

'Where is it?' Hana asked, her mouth full of a ham and egg bagel.

'Really close to where the body was found. Less than a ten minute walk, quicker in a car.'

'So this is someone who knew her, you think?' Hana asked Luke.

'Horrible to say, but yes I hope so. Quicker to find and easier to reassure the public once this does get out.'

———

It was a quiet drive back towards the east end of London and the street that Hana and Luke turned onto looked like every other in this neighbourhood. Each street was a neat row of semi-detached houses that were three stories tall, having been built to house the working class a century ago instead of the grander houses you found in London the further west and north you went.

They pulled up outside number 16 and stared at it from the car.

'She lives in Flat B, so I'd guess that's the top two floors. These houses would have been divided into flats years ago,' Hana said.

'It's been awhile since we've done this,' Luke said.

'I know. I really hate it. We have support officers on standby should we need them. I hate not knowing what we are walking into.'

Luke pursed his lips and exhaled and then took a deep breath in.

'Okay,' he said, opening the car door.

The front garden wasn't tended and a bicycle was locked to the iron railing that led up two steps to the front door. Hana pressed the button for Flat B and they waited.

It was a good minute before they heard footsteps echoing off creaking stairs inside the house. A latch was turned and there was the sound of a door opening and then another latch was turned and the door in front of them swung inwards. A young woman in her early twenties was standing there in yoga leggings and an oversized pink sweatshirt, her hair pulled back in a ponytail.

'Oh, sorry,' she said. 'I thought you were someone else.'

'Who did you think it was?' asked Hana.

The young woman stared at them, no answer forthcoming as she tried to work out who these two people were, standing on her doorstep unannounced on a Saturday morning.

'I'm Detective Chief Inspector Luke Wiley, and this is my

partner, Detective Sargeant Hana Sawatsky. Does Emma Jones live here?'

'That's who I thought you were,' the woman said.

'So she lives here?' Hana asked.

'Yes. What is this about?'

'We'd like to speak with you about Emma. May we come inside to do that? Is there anyone else in the house with you?' said Luke.

'No, I'm on my own at the moment. Our other flatmate is out.'

Hana smiled encouragingly at the woman, who suddenly looked frightened, as if she had done something wrong.

'We won't be too long,' Hana said, which she knew was a small white lie.

'Uh, I guess,' the woman said and moved aside to let the detectives in. She shut the front door and pointed past the door of Flat A towards the stairs.

'We live up here. Would you close the door behind you?'

Luke and Hana did as instructed and followed the woman up the stairs into a small open plan kitchen and living room. The space was too small for a dining table but French doors opening onto a Juliet balcony that overlooked the garden to the back and several large potted plants that liked the light in the room made it feel warm and comfortable.

'May we sit down for a moment?' Luke asked. 'Perhaps you could join us?'

The woman sat on the sofa and Hana sat next to her. Luke sat in the only other available place in the room, a battered blue chair that looked like it had perhaps been picked up off the street with a sunny yellow blanket draped over its back to cover the wear and tear.

'What's your name?' he asked.

'Rachel Champion.'

'Rachel, I'm very sorry to tell you that we are here with

upsetting news. We found the body of a young woman in the canal very close to here this morning and we believe that it is Emma. Do you have a photograph of Emma that we could take a look at?'

'What?' Rachel said. 'Are you sure?'

'It would really help us if you had a photo of her. Do you have one?' Hana gently prodded.

'Um, yes, yes.'

Rachel picked up the mobile phone that was in front of her on the coffee table and fumbled to get it to recognize her face. Her hands were shaking as she swiped her thumb across the screen.

'Here,' she said. 'I took this last week.'

Rachel held the phone out in front of her, unsure of who to give it to. Luke reached forward and took it from her and smiling back at him was Emma Jones.

# EIGHT

Hana had stepped into the stairwell to relay the news to the Incident Room. The photograph of Emma Jones taken last week was emailed over and Hana asked for the Victim Support Team to make their way over. Rachel was extremely upset.

Luke had offered to make three cups of tea and was presently trying to find spoons and cups in the tiny kitchen. Rachel was sitting on the sofa, quietly crying and Luke was doing his best to put her at ease, asking questions about her life, in order to get the girl to calm down. So far he had established that she had just finished a graduate degree in marketing, had secured a newish job with a telecommunications company and worked from home on Fridays.

Hana slipped back into the flat and smiled at Rachel.

'Thanks for the photograph. You have been so helpful. We'll have someone here that you can talk to in about an hour, okay?'

'Thanks,' Rachel said, wiping her face with the sleeve of her sweatshirt.

Luke balanced all three cups of tea in his hands and brought them to the sofa.

'Thanks,' Rachel said again.

'We are going to need some details from you, Rachel. Very basic, so nothing to worry about,' Luke said.

'Okay.'

'Do you know where Emma's family are located?'

'Not exactly. She said that they were up north. Maybe around Leeds? I'm not sure.'

'So Emma was from the Leeds area?' Hana asked.

'No. She didn't have that kind of accent. She grew up in the suburbs around here and then her parents and her sister moved up north. She went up to visit them a couple of weeks ago for the weekend.'

'Okay, that's really helpful, Rachel. Do you remember what their names are?'

Rachel shook her head.

'I don't think she ever said what her parents are called. But she talked a lot about her older sister. Her name is Caitlin.'

'Do you know how much older she is?' Hana asked.

'Two years.'

'So they would have the same last name?'

'I would assume so.'

Both Luke and Hana were thinking the same thing. It was still going to take some time to find the family with such a common last name.

Rachel sipped her tea and began to calm down now that she felt she was able to help them.

'She talked about her sister a lot, but never really about her parents.'

'That's okay, Rachel. We'll find them. Did Emma have a boyfriend?' Luke asked.

'Or a girlfriend?' Hana interrupted.

Rachel shook her head.

'Are you sure? Any chance there was someone that you didn't know about, or she just hadn't told you yet?'

'There's no way. We are so close. She would totally have told me.'

Information was pieced together from what Rachel was able to tell them. Emma had moved into the flat just over four months earlier and had taken the smallest of the three bedrooms. She was twenty one years old and worked at the local community centre.

'I think it's administrative work? Or maybe she helps out in the cafeteria there? I'm not really sure,' Rachel said. 'She is saving up to go back to school. She wants to be a teacher.'

'Could we see her room, please?'

Rachel stood up and walked towards the back of the house past her own bedroom and a small, but immaculate bathroom.

'Emma's in here.'

Rachel stood just outside the door to Emma's room, as if she didn't want to let the detectives inside.

'We aren't going to touch anything at this point, Rachel. But we need to have a look around.'

She nodded and went back towards the kitchen, leaving Luke and Hana to it.

The room was very small and only fit a single bed, a desk and another small dressing table with a mirror on it. There was no closet, but a clothes rack that was tucked into the corner of the room.

For such a dull day outside with its drizzle of rain, the room was incredibly bright. The roof sloped down over it and in addition to the window that faced the house to its right, there was a skylight directly over Emma's bed.

Her bed was unmade but the rest of the room was tidy. It looked as though she had only moved in a couple of weeks ago as there weren't many clothes on the rack, no stack of books next to the bed, no magazines or plants or candles anywhere.

'No photographs,' Hana said to Luke as she looked around.

'She's twenty one years old. They're probably all on her phone.'

'Mmm, maybe. But nothing of her family? I don't like my family and even I have a couple of framed photos in my flat.'

There wasn't much else to look at without proper equipment and the forensic team. No drawers could be opened, nothing could be picked up.

'Anything else strike you, Hana?'

Hana took a moment to reply, struggling to find the words.

'It's sort of...I don't know. Adolescent.'

'What do you mean?'

'I mean, it feels like the decor of someone still at school. It doesn't really fit with the person Rachel was describing. Look at what is on the walls.'

Luke scanned the little room and shrugged his shoulders.

'You weren't ever a teenage girl.'

'Helpful, Hana.'

'Look,' she pointed to the wall next to the clothes rack where a cheap poster of Van Gogh's sunflowers was stuck up with sticky tack, their round gummy shapes in each corner visible through the paper.

'This kind of poster is something you put up to be, I don't know, sophisticated when you are that age. And these are cut out carefully from a fashion magazine,' Hana said, pointing to a few glossy pieces of paper stuck in the same way on the wall next to Emma's bed. Skinny women in slightly outrageous dresses, tall high heeled boots and bright lipstick stared back at the detectives.

The room didn't feel like it matched the young, ambitious woman that Rachel had just described. Something was off,

Hana felt, but she couldn't quite narrow down what it was exactly.

'Let's get forensics in here and head back to see what Rowdy's got,' Luke said.

'Agreed.'

Luke and Hana rejoined Rachel in the living space and waited with her for the support officers to arrive. The poor girl was still very shaken and the inevitable questions came out of her mouth.

'Do you really think she was murdered?'

'Yes,' Luke said. 'I'm afraid so.'

'Am I in danger, too?'

'No, no. That is extremely unlikely. We don't know what happened, but we will get this person as quickly as we can.'

'Your other flat mate. Where is he?'

'He's been away for over a week. He's in Spain with his boyfriend.'

So probably not a suspect then, Hana and Luke thought simultaneously.

'And can I ask,' Hana said, 'if Emma had any problems with money? Did she struggle to pay her rent or anything like that?'

'Definitely not. I mean, not yet. She doesn't have to pay anything yet,' Rachel said.

'What do you mean?'

'Emma paid six months up front when she moved in.'

Luke and Hana looked at each other. How does a twenty one year old girl have six months rent to hand over?

'That's why we chose her,' Rachel explained. 'A lot of people came and looked at her room when we listed it. But we thought it was safer to choose the person who had the money. And then...she was so amazing...'

The tears started again and Hana shifted closer to her and put her hand on the girl's back.

'Do you know where she got this money from?' Hana asked, very gently.

'I think from her parents. I don't know. I think there was something wrong with her family.'

'What do you mean?'

'I think they were rich, but really strict or something. Like, Emma didn't have certain things growing up. It was so obvious, even though she never wanted to talk about it.'

'What sort of things?' Luke asked.

'When she moved in here, she had just got a mobile phone and I'm not sure she had ever had one before. She didn't know how to use certain things on it. Like WhatsApp. We have a group chat for the flat on WhatsApp and I had to put it on Emma's phone and show her how to use it.'

'Anything else like this?'

'I'm not sure she went out a lot. She really wanted to go clubbing and we went a couple of times after she moved in. But then...I don't know. We would get there and after half an hour, she would want to go. I wondered if her family was really religious or something? And she felt guilty? I don't know.'

The bell for Flat B buzzed and the officers were there. Luke and Hana walked down the stairs to let them in.

'Luke,' Hana said. 'We've got to find these parents.'

# NINE

The Victim Support Officers were briefed at the door by Luke and Hana and then escorted upstairs to meet Rachel.

Luke hung back for a moment, walked to the pavement and then turned back to look at the house. A shadow seemed to move in the window of Flat A, the flat below Emma and Rachel. Luke stared at the window for a moment, willing the shadow to reappear but he saw nothing.

He walked to the right and down the small weed infested alley space between the house and the one to its right. The window on the ground floor that belonged to Flat A had iron anti-theft bars across it, like all of the others on the street. The curtains were drawn. Continuing along the side of the house, Luke came to a wooden gate. He reached across the top of it and opened the latch from the other side, letting himself into the garden. A fence ran down each side of the garden, dividing the space from its adjoining neighbours. It was relatively tidy for a garden with a rectangular wooden table and four chairs that wouldn't be getting any use as winter approached.

Unusually for London, the back of the garden didn't

adjoin other gardens of the houses of the street behind it, but a laneway and several parking garages. The garage of this house was empty.

Luke looked at the house from the garden. He could see Hana and Rachel and the officers inside talking through the upper floor window. Directly below it was a smaller window and backdoor of Flat A. There was a light on so that shadow certainly belonged to someone.

Luke walked up to the backdoor and knocked. He stepped back and looked up at everyone upstairs, noting the close proximity of the two flats. These neighbours probably were aware of each others' business.

Luke knocked again.

Not getting any answer, Luke went back around the front and up to the buzzer of Flat A. He pressed it, and kept his thumb on it a beat longer than necessary.

There was no answer.

Luke pounded his fist on the inside door of Flat A.

'Metropolitan Police.'

Still no answer.

Luke walked back up the stairs to where everyone was sitting in the living room.

'Rachel, do you know your neighbour downstairs?'

'Nick? Sort of.'

'What do you think of him?'

'Um,' Rachel said. 'He's fine. I mean, I doubt he would have had anything to do with this. He's nice. We've never had a problem with him.'

'Does he live there alone?'

'Yes. He works from home. He does tech support or something. He always takes in our packages for us if we're not in.'

'Was he friendly with Emma?'

'I guess so. But they weren't, like, friends. Same as with

me. We say *hi* when we pass each other. He leaves our packages outside our inner door downstairs. That's about it.'

Hana looked quizzically at Luke and he stepped up to move into the stairwell, motioning her to follow him.

'What's up?'

'He's in there. I knocked at both the front and back door, but he's not answering.'

Hana pressed a button on her mobile and brought it up to her ear.

'Rowdy? Can you see what you can bring up on whoever lives at Flat A here?'

There was a pause as she listened to the other end of the line.

'Thanks.'

'What do you want to do here?' she asked.

'I'd like to know why this guy isn't answering the door when there are police upstairs at the flat of a girl who was found murdered in the canal ten minutes down the road this morning.'

'I'll see if I can rouse him. Why don't you wait out back in case. We'll double team him.'

'Old school,' said Luke. 'I'm on it.'

Luke and Hana headed downstairs and Hana waited for Luke to creep around the back and ease himself as quietly as he could through the gate. He hovered by the fence to the right, making sure he couldn't be seen from any window in the house.

Luke heard Hana hammering on the door and announcing herself. She pounded on the door again and instructed whoever was inside to open the door.

The sound of a creaking door easing itself open was barely audible and Luke moved swiftly towards it. The man looked his way just as Luke reached for him and instead of ducking out of Luke's grasp, he leaned towards Luke with the full weight of his body, slamming into him.

A sharp stab of pain shot through Luke's jaw exactly where the bastard had made contact with his shoulder and he staggered to the ground. It was just the split second needed for the neighbour to bolt. He was across the grass as Luke jumped to his feet and sprinted after him.

*Fuck*, Luke thought as he tried to ignore the pain radiating across his collarbone.

They were both through the garage and into the alleyway, Luke just a couple of paces behind.

*I'm too old for this.*

The guy was fast. And crucially, he knew where he was going. At the end of the lane, he turned right towards the bigger road, which Luke thought was an odd choice. But he darted through the traffic that had filtered off the motorway and leapt into the grounds of Victoria Park. Luke looked both ways in order to not be killed by the oncoming traffic and jumped over the metal barrier that separated the park from the road.

Nick the neighbour was nowhere to be seen.

*Goddamit*, Luke hissed.

His mobile phone was still miraculously in his pocket and he pulled it out as he began to walk back towards the house. He took a couple of moments to catch his breath and then dialled the station.

Rowdy found who he wanted to talk to and put him on the line.

'Take this number down,' Luke instructed. 'It's mine. I want you to call this number and no one else. Do you understand? Now, do you have any civilian clothing with you?'

Luke closed his eyes. Nothing was easy today.

'Fine. Either borrow something or go and buy something to put on, whatever is faster. I'm going to give you an address and I need you to monitor the entrances at the front and back. You're going to want to spend 90% of your time at the back entrance. Don't be seen. The guy you're looking for is about 5'7" — not big. Stocky little shit. The second you see him enter his flat, you call me.'

Luke rubbed his collarbone and winced.

'Parker, don't let me down.'

# TEN

Back at Scotland Yard, Rowdy was coming up blank except for the details of Emma Jones' bank account.

'Luke, this account was only opened four and a half months ago. With a cash deposit of £10,000. Apart from some cash that was withdrawn, the first transaction is a withdrawl of £3900 to a Rachel Champion.'

'That's the six month deposit for the flat share. And after that?'

'It looks like regular spending, although not a lot of it. Some cheap clothing stores, some groceries, a pay as you go mobile phone. Amazon. A couple of pubs. Things like that. There is a regular payment from Hackney Administrative Council and then three other deposits of differing amounts from three separate accounts. They look like personal accounts.'

'I'm going to need those names.'

'Already on it.'

'Can you talk to the bank about this initial deposit? Or is there a paper trail that leads to this account being opened? From another bank branch or something?'

'I've already done that. There's nothing. You don't need to provide detail of the origin of a cash deposit at that level. And the account was opened with PASS card.'

'What the hell is that?' Luke asked.

'If you don't have a driver's license or a passport, you can get a PASS card from the post office and it acts as official identification. You can actually get it online. Emma would have also needed proof of address for the bank account, and the PASS card would have been posted somewhere. I'm going to guess that it's the same address. You'll have it as soon as I do.'

'Thanks, Rowdy.'

'You're not going to be pleased with what's happening next door.'

She nodded her head towards the back of the Serious Crimes Unit.

'Oh god, what now?'

Before Rowdy could answer, Luke's mobile rang and it was Hana. He motioned another thank you to Rowdy and stepped out to take the call back in his office. As he walked down the hall he saw the one thing he didn't want to see.

Journalists.

*Fuck.*

The rage didn't simmer in Luke Wiley so much as immediately boil over, like a pot of water on an induction stove top. He was so distracted that he realized he wasn't properly listening to his partner on the other end of the line.

'Hana, I'm sorry. Can you repeat that?'

Hana, still at Emma and Rachel's flat with the forensics team, had been examining everything in Emma's room.

'There's just not a lot here, Luke. No laptop, so she might have had that with her. But absolutely nothing that indicates what her background is or where she was living before here. And I've gone through her social media accounts with Rachel.

They are all brand new and she mostly follows celebrities. Something's not right here.'

'Okay, thanks. And something's not right here, either. I see goddamn Toby Peacock down the hall.'

'Oh no, Luke. You've got to be kidding.'

'Not even remotely. See you when you're back.'

'Luke, don't...'

Luke hung up the call before Hana could talk him down from what he was about to do. He headed in the direction of the high pitched whiny voice that he had forgotten how much he hated.

Toby Peacock was rather true to his name. He had somehow risen to the position of Deputy Editor of The Star, the kind of publication that you wouldn't really call a newspaper because the philosophy behind the news they printed favoured the more sordid the better approach.

Toby Peacock relied on click bait to get his readers' attention and you had the feeling that he didn't do it just for his bottom line. He did it because he enjoyed it.

'Well, well, if I didn't see it with my own eyes,' Peacock said as Luke approached him. 'I heard you were back at the Met but I couldn't believe it. Got bored of your private jet already, Wiley?'

Luke bit the inside of his cheek so hard that he could sense the metallic taste of blood. He extended his hand and Peacock flinched slightly, unsure if he was about to be slapped or if he should extend his own for a handshake. He decided to simply stand there.

'A pleasure as usual,' Luke offered. 'I don't have anything to say to you at this point, except to ask who called you.'

'Sources, sources,' Peacock sneered. 'Can't say I'm afraid.'

'I wouldn't go believing everything you've been told. You can never be sure who's telling the truth around here if they're busy speaking to the press instead of working.'

'Who is she, Wiley? Do you have an ID on the body? Is there a killer on the loose?'

Luke craned his neck around this irritating, preening man to catch the eye of anyone else. He spotted a junior sergeant, just about to clock off for the day.

'You,' Luke pointed at her. 'Would you be so kind as to escort Mr. Peacock out? Out of the building, to be clear.'

'Sir,' she nodded and waited for Peacock to join her by the lift.

Peacock was still prattling on as Luke headed back towards the Incident Room, the not so gentle goading from the journalist audible to most of the floor.

Luke shut the door to the Incident Room behind him and walked up to the board and picked up a pen. As there was nothing more to add to the dead girl's identity, he wrote only two words in block letters above her name.

NO LEAKS

He turned to face the room.

'Do we understand each other?'

Half a dozen solemn faces stared back at him and looked at each person individually. They all looked right back at him.

The leak didn't come from inside this room. He should have known.

'Emma Jones was twenty one years old. She had her whole life ahead of her and we think she may have been running from something, or someone. She was trying to start again. Imagine yourself at twenty one years old. How did you want to reinvent yourself? What dreams did you have? Hers were extinguished last night. Think about that before you open your mouth to anyone outside of this room.'

'Sir,' a voice said from closest to the board at the front of the room.

'Yes...' Luke realized he didn't know this young man's name.

'Sharma, Sir. Bobby Sharma. Technology Intelligence.'

'Yes, Sharma.'

'I've run some facial recognition software with a photo of the deceased's face that Dr. Chung has passed along from the lab. She hasn't popped up in any social media profile, which is slightly odd for her age.'

'I agree, Sharma. But good work. Who sent you over to be part of the team?

'Rowdy, Sir.'

Luke smiled.

'As forensics continues to go through everything both at the scene and at Emma's flat, go through everything with eyes wide open. The smallest detail could be the key. Nothing is too small to mention. And for god's sake, order in some food. I'm starving.'

# ELEVEN

Hana was displeased when she arrived back at Scotland Yard. Burgers had been ordered for the team and the only one remaining was the vegetarian option.

'This is a halloumi burger. You want me to eat a halloumi burger?'

Everyone looked a bit apologetic.

'Can someone please get Sargeant Sawatsky a Diet Coke?' Luke said, doing his best not to smile.

She opened the paper wrapper and pulled the brioche lid off the blocks of cheese and looked at it.

'And hot sauce,' she shouted to Sharma who had stepped out to find her drink. 'Find me some hot sauce!'

Hana pushed the burger away from her and looked at the board. It was basically as blank as when she left left it earlier that morning.

'We should be farther than this by now,' she said.

'Tomorrow will be a better day. Rowdy will have much more for us. Lab results will be back. We'll get him.'

'I don't like this, Luke. It's not making sense to me.

There's just nothing on this girl. What twenty one year old is so opaque? And why would the killer strangle her and then dump her in the canal. Forensics didn't find any sign of a struggle anywhere near where she went into the water. It's quite an effort to move a body once you've already killed her.'

The evening was a frustrating one for everyone in the room and eventually Luke sent them all home.

'Do you want to head off as well?' Luke asked Hana.

'What are you going to do?'

'Try to get some sleep. I have the feeling tomorrow is going to be a long day,' Luke said as he began switching off the lights in the Incident Room.

The two detectives were putting on their jackets when the screen of Luke's phone came to life, the only source of light in the dark room. It was a mobile phone number that neither of them recognized.

'Hello?'

'Sir, it's Parker. Your friendly neighbour has come home.'

'Parker. You genius. Do not let him out of your sight and do not let him leave the house again. Sawatsky and I are on our way.'

'I don't think he'll be going anywhere, Sir.'

'Why is that?'

'I've got him. Cuffed. We're currently sitting in his back doorway. I haven't entered the premises, Sir, but had the feeling that you may wish to. You know, on your own.'

Hana, who was standing on her tip toes and had her head right up to the phone so she could hear, lowered herself and had a look on her face that Luke didn't see very often. She was impressed.

'Don't make any noise. And keep him quiet. We will be right there.'

Luke tossed the car keys to Hana.

'You drive faster.'

———

Hana had switched on the lights and siren for the best part of their drive through the east end of London and traffic had swiftly moved out of their way. About half a mile out, she switched off the siren. As they got to the intersection where the bastard had jumped the barrier into Victoria Park, she turned off the lights.

They silently pulled up down the road and approached the house on foot. The lights to Emma and Rachel's flat were out. She had clearly gone to stay elsewhere tonight and who could blame her. The lights to the house on the other side of the alleyway were also off. It was unlikely that any scuffle between Parker and Nick the neighbour had been heard.

'Oh Jesus,' Hana said, as they walked through the wooden gate and came into view of the back door.

Parker was practically sitting on top of the guy, his long legs stretched out with his feet firmly in the doorframe.

'Good evening, Sir.'

Luke and Hana stood on either side of Parker and the man he was practically holding prisoner and lifted them both up.

Luke took a good look at the guy who had bodychecked him so hard, the left side of his body was still aching.

'I'm Detective Chief Inspector Luke Wiley. I believe we met earlier when you slammed me to the ground.'

The man blinked at him.

'This is my partner, DS Sawatsky and you are already acquainted with Officer Parker. May we come inside and speak to you? Oh great, thanks,' Luke said as he barged into the house. He took a moment to adjust to the darkness and then pulled on a pair of latex gloves. Luke flipped on the lightswitch by the back door and beckoned the others inside.

'Your name, please?'

'Nicholas Tuft.'

'Nick, why didn't you open the door when we knocked this morning? We were pretty persistent. And more importantly, why did you run?'

'I don't know.'

'Poor answer, Nick. Try again.'

'Why are you here?'

'Officer Parker, you can uncuff him. Nick, why don't you take a seat somewhere a little more comfortable and we'll have a chat,' Luke said.

Parker did as instructed and Nick eased himself off the floor and looked warily at the detectives. He didn't move.

'Can I get a glass of water?' he said.

'Officer Parker will get one for you. Here,' Luke said, tossing Parker a pair of latex gloves.

'What are you doing? What are you looking for?' Nick asked.

Hana led the man towards the large desk that took up an entire wall of the ground floor. She spun the ergonomic office chair around and gestured for Nick to sit down.

'Why did you run this morning, Nick?' she asked.

'There were police officers everywhere here this morning. I didn't know what was going on. I was frightened. I just ran.'

'Where did you run to?'

'Nowhere. I mean, I went to the park and then I wandered around for a bit. Then I came home.'

'How well do you know your upstairs neighbours?'

Nick shifted in his chair and looked at the wall behind Luke.

'I know them. I mean, we live next to each other and say hi and stuff like that.'

'How well do you know Emma Jones?'

Nick opened his mouth and hesitated ever so slightly before answering. Both Luke and Hana noticed it.

'Not very well. Really just as neighbours. She hasn't been living upstairs for very long.'

'You know how long she's been living above you though?' Hana asked.

Nick remained silent.

Hana was slowly taking in the space around them. It was sparsely decorated and nothing particularly personal. The walls were bare except for a large mirror. Two computer monitors hummed quietly on the desk behind where Nick was sitting. The kitchen counter held quite a few expensive looking pieces of equipment, neatly ordered in a row.

A sofa sat along the remaining wall and in front of it was a glass coffee table where two used wine glasses were sitting. Next to them was a cardboard delivery box that had been opened and emptied of its contents. Hana pulled her jacket sleeve over her fingers and flipped it over so she could see the address label.

The name on the label was Emma Jones.

# TWELVE

For once, Luke slept soundly. After Nick Tuft was properly arrested and handcuffed and escorted by a rather proud Officer Parker back to the station to await questioning, Luke and Hana decided to call it a night.

Figuring they would get more out of the suspect after a night spent sweating in the interrogation room at the Serious Crime Unit, the two detectives had both gone home.

Luke had arrived back at his house in Islington and poured himself a glass of red wine. He had planned to do as he always did in the evening and settle down at the kitchen table to look over more files that may provide answers to Sadie's mysterious death, but instead he found himself sinking into the sofa in their sitting room. He connected his phone to the bluetooth speaker and pressed a jazz playlist. Luke didn't know anything about jazz except that he liked it and it was something he liked to listen to when he wanted to switch off. He realized that he had spent a day with his adrenaline surging through his body and finally they had a lead with the downstairs neighbour. He let himself relax.

When he finally went to bed about an hour later he did something that he had not done in a very long time. He set the alarm on his phone. And it was his alarm that woke him the next morning.

Luke had a good feeling about the day ahead. Walking onto the seventh floor at eight o'clock in the morning, a large coffee in his hand, he could see Hana was already at her desk. They were going to get this guy. They were going to put this case to bed today, he could feel it. When Luke and Hana finally found the family of Emma Jones they were going to be able to say to them that they had him.

'Morning,' Luke said.

'Hey,' Hana replied, stifling a yawn.

'What time did you come in?'

'Around six. I had hoped that we had the paperwork to seize Nick Tuft's laptop and Sharma offered to come in early and take a look at it. I thought I'd come in and keep him company, but we don't have sign off yet. Another couple of hours, apparently.'

'That's...weirdly friendly of you.'

'Right?'

The two detectives smiled at each other, and for both of them, it felt like it was before. Before Sadie died, before the mistakes of the Marcus Wright case, before they questioned everything that had happened to them. This is how they used to be. They came to work feeling buoyant, feeling ready to take on the tough stuff in front of them. They were confident. It pissed a lot of people in their office off, but this is how DCI Wiley and DS Sawatsky operated. And they felt, even with so many questions lingering, that maybe they were back to their best.

'Is O'Donnell in yet?'

'What do you think?'

'Perfect. Shall we have a little chat with Mr. Tuft?'

Nick Tuft looked dreadful. Even though Luke's collarbone was still aching and within another twenty four hours would be sporting a nasty, purple bruise, he felt a twinge of pity for him.

'Can we get you a coffee, Nick?'

'Yes, please.'

His voice was very quiet, shaking slightly and hoarse. He had been crying.

This wasn't a great sign. Crying from fear and crying from remorse happened a lot in this interrogation room and neither of them led to anything positive. Luke and Hana would have to tread carefully.

'I'm sorry that you've been in here overnight. It's not exactly comfortable, but I can assure you that you had a better night here than had you been locked up in the general holding rooms we have in Wandsworth.'

'Thank you.'

*Thank you?* He was thanking the detectives about to interrogate him? Also not a good sign.

There was a soft knock on the opaque panel of glass that faced the the rest of the Serious Crime Unit. Luke had pressed the switch to ensure the glass was opaque from both sides, so there was not a flock of people watching this interview from the other side. But he didn't let Nick know this.

Hana stood up and opened the door, accepting two steaming cups of coffee from Sharma.

She gently closed the door with her foot, placed one cup in front of Nick and the other one in front of Luke.

'We aren't going to rush this, Nick. So you take your time with your answers, okay?' She said.

Nick nodded gratefully at her, and sipped his coffee.

'How long have you lived in your flat?'

'I've been there for six years.'

The detectives already knew this, as Rowdy had pulled up the land transaction records and they could see his flat purchase just over six years ago. It was a good start that Nick was telling the truth.

'And when did you first meet Emma Jones?'

He looked like he was thinking hard about his answer.

'I guess she moved in about three months ago? It was summer. This summer just gone.'

'And how well do you know her?'

Again, Nick hesitated, like he didn't know how much information he should be giving the detectives.

'Emma and I are friends. We hang out occasionally.'

'What do you two do when you hang out?' Hana asked.

'Look,' Nick said, leaning forward in his chair. 'I'm very happy to talk about this. I think there has been a mistake. I'm not sure who said something, I really doubt it was Emma, but if it is I'm more than happy to talk to her. I really didn't know and I'm not sure that it's technically wrong.'

Luke and Hana said nothing.

'She's incredibly sweet. I really like Emma but I know that everything is not exactly as it seems. But this is not at all my fault.'

Luke could feel the optimism of his day rapidly fading away. He had no idea what this guy was talking about.

'We only slept together once,' Nick said. 'I promise you that it was completely consensual. She kind of pursued me. It was afterwards that she got all upset.'

'When did you sleep together?' Hana asked.

'A couple of weeks ago.'

'Not two nights ago? On Thursday?'

'No, absolutely not.'

Nick shook his head several times and waved his hands in

front of them, as if to emphasize that he did not sleep with Emma the night she died.

'But you saw Emma that night,' Luke said.

'Yes, after what happened a couple of weeks ago, she wanted to talk to me. We had a glass of wine. That was it. It was an impromptu thing. I texted her to say that I'd taken in a parcel for her and she came over.'

'I'd think you'd better tell us about what happened a couple of weeks ago.'

Nick was almost frantic in his earnestness. He and Emma had become friendly, chatting when they saw each other coming in and out of the house, hanging out in the garden in the summer when it was still quite hot. She had been both chatty and shy, asked lots of questions, wanted to hear his opinion of things. There had been some flirting.

Two weeks earlier, she had texted to see if he was around and Nick took that as a sign of interest. He had been correct. Emma had come downstairs and after an hour or two of chatting and watching tv, they had slept together.

'But she began to cry straight afterwards. I didn't understand what was wrong and kept asking her. She got more and more upset, really sobbing and I didn't know what to do. I was worried that I had hurt her somehow. And that's when she told me. But she begged me not to tell the others. She didn't want her flatmates to know. And I promised her that I wouldn't.'

Luke and Hana were rigid, waiting to hear the missing piece of their puzzle.

'What did she tell you?' Hana was almost whispering.

'Look, I really didn't know. I'm so sorry if Emma is upset.'

Hana and Luke were silent.

'She told me that it had been her first time and that she was only eighteen.'

Nick shifted in his chair and his eyes were darting back and forth between Luke and Hana, looking for some kind of sign. Some kind of absolution.

There was another knock on the glass — this time it was loud.

'Jesus,' Luke muttered under his breath.

Hana's chair screeched on the linoleum floor as she pushed it back to see what the badly timed interruption was for. Luke turned to look behind him and it was Rowdy at the door. She motioned for him to step outside.

Frustrated, he shook his head at Rowdy as if to say: Not now.

'Detective Chief Inspector Wiley,' Rowdy said in reply.

Rowdy never addressed him like this and Hana turned to move back inside the interrogation room.

'You too, DS Sawatsky.'

Luke looked at Nick Tufts, who was running his still shaking hands through his hair and shifting in his seat. Picking up his mug of hot coffee, Luke stood up and walked out into the hallway.

'Let's speak in your office please, Luke,' Rowdy said.

'What the hell, Rowdy? This is not the time.'

Rowdy ignored them and headed down to Luke's office, the two detectives had no choice but to follow her. Once inside, Rowdy shut the door behind them. She was holding a piece of paper in her hands.

'Are you about to make a goddamn speech or something?' Luke hissed. 'We were in the middle of something that really can't wait.'

'Neither can this, Luke.'

Rowdy glanced at the piece of paper in her hands again and opened her mouth. She took a breath and hesitated.

'We've got the DNA results back from the lab. They just came in. Luke, the woman in the canal is not Emma Jones.'

'What do you mean?'

The moment that Rowdy told Luke who it was, he dropped his mug of coffee and it shattered into hundreds of pieces.

# Thirteen

Hana wasn't looking at Rowdy. She was staring at Luke and the look on her face was one of complete incredulity.

'Well, that was dramatic.'

Luke and Rowdy said nothing. They simply stared at each other.

'Would someone like to tell me what's going on?'

Luke ignored the shattered mug that now lay scattered over most of his office floor and stepped towards Rowdy to take the piece of paper out of her hand. The shards of ceramic crunched under his feet.

'I can have Dr. Chung run it again, but I'm not sure we're going to get a different result.'

'We don't need to run it again,' Luke said, very softly.

'We found her, Luke.'

'Not in time.'

'I'm sorry. But her family will know now.'

Luke could only nod. Hana slowly realized that whatever this was, it was enormous. The unspoken words hanging in the air of Luke's office were heavy and sad. She didn't ask any other questions. Although Hana was desperate to understand what had just happened, she knew that when she was eventually told, the story would be a devastating one. She could see it plain as day on the faces of her partner and Laura Rowdy.

The ceramic crunched under Luke's feet again as he moved to collect his jacket that had been tossed onto his desk in his optimistic mood just half an hour earlier.

'Rowdy, you should have Nick Tuft released under caution. We're going to need a lot of information out of him, but I don't think he's our guy. Get Forensics on standby to go through her room again. We will have missed something because we didn't know what we were looking for. And I'm sorry about this.' He gestured at the shards of white coffee mug and pools of brown liquid that now covered his office floor.

Rowdy waved her hands and told him not to worry about it. She'd get it cleaned up.

'Come on, Hana. We have to go.'

Luke and Hana walked down the hall towards the lift and Hana noticed how Luke's gait wasn't rushed. It felt resigned — the complete opposite of how he had walked into the office earlier that morning.

'Luke,' Rowdy suddenly called out.

Hana and Luke turned towards her as the doors to the lift opened.

'Say hi to her for me,' she said. 'She'll want to come back.'

Luke simply nodded and the doors closed in front of them.

# FOURTEEN

'Her name is Grace Feist,' Luke said after they had pulled out of the parking garage underneath Scotland Yard and had maneuvered down the Embankment towards the south east of the city.

'I know that name. I know who Grace Feist is. A lot of the specifics escape me, though.'

'Yes,' Luke said. 'It was just before your time — it all happened about two years before we met.'

'Where are we going, Luke?'

'Sussex. There is someone who has to be told before anyone else.'

'Grace's family lives in Sussex?'

'No.'

———

Grace Feist had been twelve years old when it happened. The playing fields in the north end of London above Hampstead Heath were busy on a Saturday in May. Grace was there with her family because her sister, two years younger, was in a football tournament. The weather had just tipped from the indecisiveness of spring into the first gloriously warm summer weekend. London always feels different on the weekend the weather shifts — slightly too excited, slightly dangerous in the pockets of nighttime socializing, as if anything could happen and those who had been cooped up all winter and through the rainy days of March and April were okay to let it happen.

But on the playing fields of North London, it was primarily families who were feeling the anticipation of summer in the air. Parents were chatting convivially to each other, picnics had been laid out and children were running around enjoying the day.

Luke had interviewed dozens and dozens of people who were there on this Saturday and they all said the same thing.

It was a lovely day. There was nothing out of the ordinary.

Grace Feist hadn't been playing football that day and she was a bit bored. She had ridden her bike over to the field, just slightly ahead of her parents and sister but within their view. Later that evening, her mother would lament over and over again that they should have driven over. If the bicycle hadn't been with them, none of this would have happened. But it was a glorious day in May and the family had walked over from their home, about a thirty minute walk, with football cleats and lunch in rucksacks on their backs.

Luke remembers the sister, Emily, who had looked so small and frightened as the events of the day unfolded. She was simultaneously in the way and also an integral part of their questioning. What did she see? Had anyone been following Grace? What was unusual about their morning? The poor girl answered as best she could and Luke finally asked her if she had won her football match that day. She had nodded and began to cry, as if her victory had somehow created the disaster unfolding in front of them. Luke had felt dreadful for her.

After the match ended, the families had milled around,

chatting and eating lunch together. Grace had been bored, as any twelve year old who felt much older than everyone else there, as you do on the cusp of adolesence. She had asked her father permission to ride her bike around the playing fields for a bit until they were all ready to go home.

He had said yes.

Luke knows that Grace's father, a kind looking man who was then in his late forties, not too much older than Luke's age now, probably thought about that moment every day of his life. How heavy the regret must hang on him.

When the Feists were ready to go, they waited a bit for Grace to return from her ride. But she did not return. As families packed up their belongings and goodbyes were made, Jamie and Rosamund Feist were annoyed. In that tricky stage where childhood begins to fall away and independence is earned and granted, Grace had pushed the boundary too far that afternoon.

Jamie said that he would head back to the house and see if Grace had returned there, too bored by the activities at the playing fields. But when he got home, his daughter was not there. Jamie tried to keep his voice calm when he called Rosamund's mobile to report that their daughter was not at home. It was in this moment that he knew something was wrong. He left a hastily scribbled note on the kitchen counter that instructed Grace to stay put when she got home and that they would be following shortly.

The note was never read.

By the time Jamie returned to the field, Rosamund had organized a few remaining parents to scour the area for Grace. Everyone came back looking slightly anxious and that is when Jamie called the police.

At first, the officers that took the call out weren't especially worried. It was that strange, beautiful weekend where London emerged into its summer state and perhaps Grace had bumped into friends and was off having fun, unaware of the situation she had left behind. But as friends and their parents were tracked down, neighbours' doors were knocked upon, and all known favourite places to ride her bike were checked and there was no sign of Grace, the mood changed abruptly. Grace Feist had gone from a fun loving girl who was perhaps misbehaving to an official missing child and by late afternoon, Luke Wiley had arrived at the Feist family home and protocols were put into place.

———

As Luke and Hana sped down the motorway towards Sussex, it was as if six years had not passed. The emotions of that day in early May and everything that came later had never left him. He gripped the steering wheel thinking about Jamie Feist in particular. His daughter's disappearance had crushed him and Luke remembered how he had taken the little moon charm from Grace's necklace, still hanging from the knob on her bedside table, and looped it over his own weathered leather necklace. He wanted to keep her as close to him as he could. He was desperate.

Grace Feist had never been found. Until her body was pulled out of the canal by Broadway Market forty eight hours earlier.

'Where was she this entire time?' Luke said, not really as a question for Hana, but voicing out loud the thoughts in his head.

'I hadn't understood that you worked this case,' she replied, quietly.

'I had just transferred to Serious Crime. None of us could believe that Grace could simply vanish.'

'Do you think she simply vanished?'

'No. She was definitely taken by someone.'

'But she seemed to be living independently in that flat with Rachel Champion for all this time. Why didn't she go home? It doesn't make sense.'

'I don't know.'

Luke shook his head. The fields of the Sussex countryside were a deep green from the autumn rain and large valleys that dipped in every direction rolled by them as the car picked up speed.

'I thought the detective on the Grace Feist case was Philippa Nicolson.'

'It was,' said Luke.

'You worked on this with Nicolson? I didn't know that.'

Hana thought back to Sadie's funeral. It was a haze of a day — all of Sadie's friends, of which there seemed to be hundreds, and their colleagues from the Met. She had found the day overwhelming. But she remembered Philippa Nicolson — she was not the kind of woman one forgets. She had been crying as she pulled Luke into an embrace at the end of the service. Hana only now understood the significance of that moment.

'She retired soon after Grace went missing, didn't she?'

'Yes,' said Luke. 'About a year later. We knew Grace had to be dead by then and Philippa took it all very badly.'

'How do you think she will react when she finds out that Grace was alive this entire time?'

'You're about to see for yourself,' said Luke, as he indicated and turned left.

# FIFTEEN

Their car drove down a country road that was dotted with large homes and even larger hedgerows. It was the kind of countryside with Michelin starred pubs and farm stands selling fresh eggs — the metal box next to them holding change for you to help yourself when leaving your money for the purchase.

They pulled off the road onto a lane that curved around a series of small greenhouses and Luke parked in front of the house. It wasn't enormous, but it felt grand, and was probably the old rectory once associated with the church that was another half mile down the road.

'I feel like I'm intruding,' said Hana.

'You're not.'

Luke smiled at her and leaned against the roof of the car, still standing in the open door.

'And I didn't want to do this alone.'

'Okay,' Hana said.

Luke hoped that Philippa was home — this wasn't the kind of news that could be delivered on the phone. He pressed the bell and heard the chime from inside the house.

After a few moments, the door swung open.

Standing there was a man in his early seventies, he was wearing an apron and drying his hands on a tea towel. It took him a moment to take in the two detectives standing at his front door.

'Luke,' he said. 'My god. Hello.'

'Hello, Richard,' Luke said, extending his hand and the two men exchanged a warm handshake.

'This is DS Hana Sawatsky.'

'Hello,' Hana said. 'Apologies for turning up unannounced.'

'Not at all,' Richard replied, leaning in to shake Hana's hand. 'But I'm guessing this is not a social visit. Come in, come in.'

Richard ushered them inside and protested as they tried to take off their shoes.

'No need,' he called out, beckoning for them to follow him down the hall. 'Let me get her. She's outside.'

Luke and Hana walked through the house, its large stone slabs in the hall covered by a well worn Persian rug. Hana could see a wood stove was lit in one of the rooms they passed that looked like a study, its heat radiating throughout the rest of the ground floor. It was cosier inside than its outward appearance suggested.

They followed Richard into the kitchen and then waited as he stepped outside. She could tell that Luke was suddenly nervous, which wasn't something Hana saw very often. He was taking deep breaths and looked like he didn't know what to do with his arms until he finally clasped his hands together behind his back.

The kitchen door opened and Richard had Philippa in tow. She looked exactly how Hana remembered her, but in gardening clothes. Her grey hair was tied back loosely and her expression, always so serious until the moment she smiled when it became warm and inviting, was maybe a tad more relaxed than it used to be.

Richard nodded at them.

'I'll leave you to it.'

Philippa didn't move to embrace Luke, but took off her gardening gloves one by one and tossed them into the kitchen sink.

'You're either here to tell me something or to ask for my help. Which is it?'

'Both, I'm afraid, Philippa.'

Philippa looked like she had been expecting them somehow, not showing any sign of being surprised or bothered by their appearance.

'Philippa, may I introduce DS Hana Sawatsky,' Luke said.

'Ma'am,' said Hana, unsure if she should step forward and shake Philippa's hand.

Philippa looked at her watch and sighed.

'Too early for a drink, I suspect. You probably need one, working with this one,' she said, nodding towards Luke.

Hana chuckled, and instantly felt herself relaxing in what had been an incredibly tense morning.

'And I'm going to need one after this, aren't I?' she continued, looking in Luke's direction.

'How about a coffee? If I remember correctly, you actually know how to brew a proper cup,' Luke said, the comment not lost on Hana.

Philippa began to busy herself with the espresso machine that sat on the kitchen counter and told them to make themselves comfortable in the study. When the three detectives were settled, Philippa poured them both a cup of coffee but left her own cup untouched on the tray she had put down on the table between them.

'Let's have it then.'

Luke took a sip and then placed his cup down. He leaned forward and cleared his throat.

'Philippa, we've found Grace Feist.'

Her intake of breath was sharp and audible. She said nothing in reply, only looking down at her lap as if she was saying a private prayer.

'You found her remains.'

'Sort of, Philippa,' said Luke. 'We pulled her body out of Regent Canal in East London on Friday morning. She had only been in the water for a few hours. DNA has confirmed it is Grace.'

At this revelation, Philippa suddenly sat bolt upright, as if she had suffered an electric shock.

'She was alive this entire time?'

'Yes.'

'Held somewhere? Do you know where?'

'That's the thing, Philippa. She wasn't being held. She was living in a flat share with two other people about a ten minute walk from where she was pulled out of the canal.'

'This can't be right.'

Luke and Philippa stared at each other. One in disbelief, the other in increasing frustration at the puzzle in front of them that didn't make any sense.

'Jamie and Rosamund?' Philippa asked.

'We haven't told them yet, Ma'am,' said Hana.

'This isn't good, this really, really isn't good,' muttered Philippa, as she stood up and walked towards the cabinet in the corner of the study.

She pulled open a drawer and began removing folders, stuffed full of papers. After pulling out what seemed like half of the bottom drawer of the cabinet, she asked Hana to empty one of the cardboard boxes in the adjacent room and bring it to her. After filling the box with the folders, Philippa looked at them both and readjusted the elastic band in her hair.

'We fucking missed something, Luke. How can we possibly go to the Feist's house, tell them their daughter is dead but that she had actually been living in London this whole time?'

'We don't know that she was in London this whole time,' he replied.

'Well, we don't know much at all, do we? Jesus Christ.'

'Philippa, we have the files in storage at Scotland Yard, you don't need to pack all of these up for us,' Luke said.

'You don't have these files, Luke. These are mine.'

Luke understood immediately.

Philippa had never let this case go. She had been working on it for the past six years, even in retirement. She didn't want to go to her own grave without finding Grace Feist and returning her to her parents.

And today was going to be the day she did this.

'We came straight here when the DNA results came in from Rowdy. Nothing else has been set up,' Luke said. 'I don't even know if the Feists are still at the same location.'

'They are,' said Philippa. 'I see them at least once a year. I...'

Philippa voice trailed off before she regained her composure.

'Luke, they have never stopped waiting for Grace to come home.'

It was at this point that Richard appeared in the doorway of the study and took in his wife's demeanour and the fact that both of the other detectives were no longer sitting down, drinking their coffees.

'I take it no one is staying for lunch?'

Philippa looked at her husband and between them was the understanding every detective's spouse had — she would be back when she could and would fill him in later but right now, she had to go.

'We'll put the box in the car. Shall we wait for you to change and get things together?' Luke asked.

'Is O'Donnell still running Serious Crime?'

Hana nodded.

'Well, then we don't have a lot of time. Luke, you'd better not still be driving at the speed of a tortoise.'

# Sixteen

The girl was groggy. She had been taken completely by surprise and her first thought was she had been stung by a wasp. The prick on the back of her thigh had been quick and sharp and she had cried out involuntarily.

The man she had been talking to looked at her with concern.

'Are you okay?'

And then her legs gave way.

The man instinctively moved forward to grab her and he was strong. He held her up with only one arm around her waist, his hand tucked into her armpit.

She felt very warm, warmer than she should even on this hot day and her second thought was that she was having an allergic reaction to the wasp sting. She had heard about this and a friend of hers at school always carried a shot of adrenaline in her pencil case. She hadn't seen the woman before now who was suddenly at her side and her hands were also helping to hold her up.

When she went to speak, she found that her mouth

wouldn't move the way she needed it to and her tongue felt big and heavy in her mouth. Her whole body felt heavy.

The man and the woman seemed able to sweep her along with them. Were her feet touching the ground? She couldn't tell.

They had a car parked right there and the woman was opening the door to the backseat. She was being eased inside.

'We're taking you to the hospital,' the man said. Or she thought he said.

*Her bike.*

She tried to tell them about her bike. They needed to bring it. Her parents would be so mad. The bike had been a birthday gift and it was such a big deal. She had picked it out with her dad. She was already late.

She sank into the backseat and the woman told her not to worry. Everything was going to be okay. The woman was stroking her hair.

She must have fallen asleep and when she woke up, she didn't understand why she was so cold. Her eyes still felt heavy and she had a headache. There was the faint taste of blood in her mouth, like she had bitten the inside of her cheek.

The room was softly lit and she realized that her bedroom curtains must be shut. She turned to look at the window and it wasn't there.

This wasn't her bedroom.

# SEVENTEEN

Philippa Nicolson had been a legend on the Serious Crime Unit at the Met. She was no nonsense, to the point, uncanny in her ability to see the missing link in a case before anyone else and, rumour had it, could drink every single man on the unit under the table.

She had refused Hana's offer of sitting in the front seat on their way back to London.

'We need to get acquainted, Sawatsky. And I'm too old to be craning my neck around to look at you back there.'

If Hana thought that the car ride would be mostly silent due to the gravity of the situation, she was completely wrong. Nicolson wanted to talk and Hana had a lot of questions.

Grace Feist had vanished without a trace. Hundreds of potential witnesses were interviewed, CCTV that covered most of the city of London was scoured over several months and there were very few leads.

Grace's bicycle had been found abandoned on the pavement that bordered the east end of the playing field. This particular area was not visible to those watching the football or using the playground. A copse of trees obscured this road from their vantage point and the pavement was next to the only road that allowed parking. The parking was free, so there was no record of any card payment associated with a number plate. And there was no CCTV.

It had felt at the time like a perfect crime. It was also national headline news. One of the first things Nicolson had asked as they pulled away from her house was how tight was the team assigned to this case.

'We've already had a leak,' Hana admitted.

'Toby Peacock was sniffing around when we pulled the body out of the canal. But there's been no ID yet, officially, so he won't have anything,' Luke said.

'Yet,' replied Nicolson.

Luke's mobile was on silent but he had looked at the screen before getting back in the car and there were half a dozen missed calls from O'Donnell. Nicolson considered what this meant before saying anything.

'I would imagine that even Stephen O'Donnell wants to tread carefully here. The Met doesn't look great. Grace Feist has been alive this entire time and suddenly she's been murdered six years later. It could appear that we stopped searching for her. Which we didn't.'

Luke agreed with her.

'We are going to have to arrange a press conference, but I'd like to look at everything one more time. And no one does anything or says a word to anyone until Jamie and Rosamund Feist are informed.'

Hana suddenly felt unsure of how to contribute, but she knew that she felt the same as Luke and Nicolson in desperately wanting to get whoever had killed Grace Feist. There was a feeling in the car that three was a crowd and as someone who never hesitated before asking a question, she felt suddenly a bit shy.

Clearing her throat and trying to not sound accusatory, she tried to get the facts straight in her head.

'We thought we had someone for Grace's kidnapping, didn't we? I will have to go back and read through all of the case notes but there was a prime suspect, right?'

'That's right,' said Nicolson. 'Witnesses saw a man who had been running around the playing fields talking to Grace along the tree line on the east side of the field. We were convinced it was him.'

'What was his name?'

In unison, Luke and Nicolson spoke in perfect unison.

'James Linton.'

'But we couldn't pin it on him,' continued Nicolson.

'And do you still think he's our guy?' asked Hana.

There was no reply from either detective.

Hana's brain felt like it was on overdrive and the speeding traffic rushing towards her on the other side of the motorway looked exactly how she felt. She had been thinking about the younger sister. What did she remember? What did she know?

Hana was particularly close to her younger sister and they were almost five years apart in age. Sisters kept secrets — it was almost a planetary rule.

'The sister, Emily,' Hana said. 'Are you sure she was two years younger than Grace?'

'Yes,' said Nicolson. 'Why?'

'We didn't get a lot out of Grace's flatmate in terms of Grace's background, but the flatmate said that she did talk a lot about her sister. But she said her sister was two years older and her name was Caitlin.'

Hana could see the puzzled look on Nicolson's face in her sideview mirror.

'What else did the flatmate say?'

'She suspected that Grace had very strict parents, maybe

religious? Grace didn't use any social media and the flatmate had to help her put apps on her mobile phone.'

Now it was Luke's turn to look in the rearview mirror to check for Nicolson's reaction. Everyone was silent for a few minutes until Nicolson finally spoke.

'It's unthinkable.'

'I know,' Luke said, quietly, navigating through the quieter streets of London as they made their way towards Hampstead Heath and the Feist home just beyond it.

'What is unthinkable?' asked Hana.

Nicolson stared out the window, as if to say that she was done talking. It was Luke who spoke.

'The possibility that Grace was kidnapped, held some-where for six years and suddenly let go two months ago.'

# Eighteen

'Do you need directions?' Nicolson asked Luke as they approached the pretty tree lined streets of Muswell Hill in north London.

'No, I remember it.'

When they had parked on the Feist's street, Luke stepped out of the car to finally ring O'Donnell and explain where they had been and what they were about to do. For once, he seemed to appreciate the difficult task — the most difficult a detective ever has to perform — and wished them luck.

'I'm glad Nicolson is there with you.'

'As am I, Stephen.'

'But when you are finished,' O'Donnell said, 'I need all three of you back at the station. I've set up a press conference for four o'clock this afternoon.'

Luke closed his eyes and was glad that he wasn't physically in the same room as O'Donnell in this moment. A press conference today was a mistake. He knew that O'Donnell would argue that they would need help from the public to track down where Grace had been over the past six years. Had she been seen somewhere? Had she ever attended school? These were answers they needed but Luke knew that the media frenzy would be fierce and unpleasant and distracting.

He looked at his watch. They had a couple of hours before the press conference, for which he knew his presence would be required.

Returning to the car, he filled Nicolson and Hana in on the details of his conversation and they knew what they had to do, but that time was tight.

Hana looked very uncomfortable.

'Shall I wait behind in the car?'

'No,' Nicolson shook her head. 'Absolutely not. We need you.'

A look of relief flooded Hana's face and Luke felt like he had suddenly jumped back in time to the days of the one year he partnered Philippa Nicolson. She could be fierce and quick to anger. Her colleagues treaded carefully around her. But she was kind and clever and knew a good detective when she saw one.

'There is something you both should know,' Nicolson said. 'Jamie Feist has had a stroke. It happened two years ago and it was a bad one. Cognitively he is absolutely the same, but he has yet to regain full function on his left hand side. So speech is slow — you will need to be patient. And he uses a wheelchair for much of the day.'

'I didn't know,' Luke said.

'You do know how close he was to Grace.'

'Yes.'

'This is going to be the worst moment of his life. We know what we need to do.'

They were perhaps meant to be fighting words, but as Philippa Nicolson walked towards the front door of the Feist home, Luke and Hana felt such dread in the pit of their stomachs that it felt hard to move.

The garden gnome that Luke remembered was still to the right hand side of the door, tucked into the lavender that had grown up and taken over what used to be a perfectly tended garden bed. The gnome had been purchased just a couple of weeks before Grace's disappearance and Jamie had spoken about it frequently. He and Grace had seen it in the garden centre and bought it as a joke because they knew that Rosamund would despise it. He said over and over that they were the same, he and Grace. He couldn't lose her. They had to find her.

Luke looked at the gnome with tremendous sadness, like it had been left in the garden as a beacon for their missing daughter. *We are still here. We are waiting for you.*

Philippa Nicolson lifted her hand to press the doorbell and it hovered there for a moment, as if she was steeling herself for what was about to happen within the next five minutes. She pressed it and the three detectives took a step back and waited.

The door was opened by Emily Feist. Now sixteen years old, almost seventeen, she looked completely different from when Luke had last laid eyes on her. But it was Luke that she seemed to notice first, his height a good foot taller than both Hana and Nicolson drawing Emily's eyes towards him. While it perhaps took Luke a moment to remember Emily, there was no such delay for the teenager.

'Luke,' she said, in astonishment.

They had, of course, Hana thought, been on a first name basis.

'Hello, Emily.'

Emily took in the three detectives standing in front of her on her doorstep and the initial surprise now over, suddenly realized that there must be an important reason for their presence.

'Come in,' she said, as she opened the door widely and let them inside.

'I'll get my mum.'

Emily disappeared up the staircase that led to the first floor from the entrance hall and the detectives waited. Luke noticed that while the house felt largely the same, the two doorways that he could see from the hall — one into the sitting room and one that led towards the kitchen at the back of the house — had been widened. It hadn't been particularly well done, with the new door frames in slightly different sizes, but he imagined that when Jamie had his stroke, all they wanted to do was get him home and as comfortable as soon as possible.

The Feist family had been through enough.

Rosamund Feist appeared at the top of the stairs and paused. She took in the three detectives standing in her front hall and she knew immediately the purpose of their unannounced visit. She gripped the banister and descended very slowly, one step at a time, as if slowing down her movement would maybe, desperately, result in a different outcome. A different reason for this visit. They all noticed that her hands were shaking.

There was no greeting.

'Let me get Jamie,' she said. 'He's in the kitchen.'

'I'll go,' Emily piped up, and she moved swiftly down the hall to get her father.

Rosamund didn't gesture to them, or say anything further. She simply walked into the sitting room and went towards the window. She turned away from the detectives and stared out towards the street.

The sound of the wheelchair rolling down the hall towards them only heightened the dread that the detectives felt. The air in the room felt very heavy. Emily clearly hadn't told her father who had arrived. The moment he saw Luke and Nicolson he began to wail.

His body shook in the chair and he pounded his one

working fist against his thigh, again and again. Although only one side of his body functioned at full strength, Jamie Feist's tears flowed evenly down both sides of his face. His moan turned to gentle sobbing and this made Emily begin to cry, too.

Luke stepped forward and leaned towards the grieving father. He did not crouch down, choosing to ignore his disability, and placed one of his hands on each of Jamie's shoulders. Luke did not speak.

Nicolson sat down on the sofa and Hana took this as her cue to do the same. Sniffling, Emily pushed her father's wheelchair to the empty space in the room, a space that had been cleared permanently for it. Luke came to join them on the remaining empty chair while Emily hovered next to her dad.

Rosamund did not move from the window, still staring out towards the darkening sky of the November afternoon. No one in the room dared to disturb her.

It was Nicolson who spoke first.

'This is Detective Sergeant Hana Sawatsky.'

Hana wanted to nod, but instead sat rigidly still.

'There is no easy way to let you know,' Nicolson said softly, 'that we have found Grace's body. We have performed a DNA test and it is Grace. There are no words to describe how sorry we are.'

At this point, Nicolson stopped. She had choked up and could not continue. Luke respected her too much to jump in. The room sat in silence for a few moments until Rosamund finally turned around to look at them.

Her tears were silent and had collected under her chin. She ignored them and did not wipe them away, but let the droplets slide slowly down her neck.

'You are sure?' she said.

Nicolson nodded.

'Where was she?'

It was such a simple question and the detectives knew that their answer was anything but simple. The Feists thought they had just received the worst news imaginable, but it was about to get so much worse.

Luke cleared his throat.

'Grace's body was found in Regent's Canal in East London on Friday morning.'

'What?' Jamie said, his eyes wild and searching.

'I know,' said Luke. 'We have the same questions, Jamie. She was in the canal but the forensic report shows that she did not have any water in her lungs. Grace did not drown. I'm so sorry but it appears that she was killed in the evening on Thursday or early Friday morning.'

Emily had sat down by this point, crouched on the floor next to her father's wheelchair.

'I don't understand,' she said. 'Grace was alive this entire time?'

'Yes,' Nicolson answered her.

'Where the hell was she?' Rosamund suddenly cried out. 'Why didn't we find her?'

'I will get you all of these answers, Rosamund. I promise you,' Nicolson said.

'We do know where she was living for the past two months,' Luke said, knowing that the tenor of the conversation was about to abruptly change.

'What do you mean?' Grace's mother asked.

'She had false identification on her when she was found. She was calling herself Emma Jones. Does this name ring any bells for you?'

The look of disbelief on the faces of all three Feist family members in the room was the same. They were as much in the dark as Hana, Luke and Nicolson.

'And she was sharing a flat with two other people — a

young woman and a young man in their early twenties — just by Broadway Market in Hackney.'

'So not with her kidnapper?' Jamie asked.

'It doesn't appear so.'

'Detectives,' Rosamund said, staring directly at her husband. 'Take us there.'

# NINETEEN

Everyone in the Incident Room on the seventh floor of Scotland Yard was a bit shellshocked. The news that Emma Jones was, in fact, Grace Feist had seemed unfathomable. When Luke and Hana returned to the team, the name EMMA JONES was still in block letters at the top of the board in Luke's handwriting.

'Sharma,' Luke said, 'why don't you go ahead and adjust our information up there.'

Bobby Sharma was surprised to be asked, but jumped up and picked up the black marker pen. He didn't erase Emma's name, but drew an arrow pointing towards the name Grace Feist, which he added to its right.

'Good lad,' said Luke. 'That's exactly right. We don't abandon the search for information on Emma Jones. It's Emma who is going to bring us to Grace's killer, and perhaps her kidnapper as well.'

'Do you think this is the same person, Sir?'

'Absolutely no idea,' said Luke. 'And that is the last time that those three words will be spoken in this room with this team. Am I understood?'

'Yes, Sir,' said every voice in the room, even Hana's.

Philippa Nicolson had remained behind with the Feists. They had refused the assistance of the Victim Support Officers, having gone through that process more times than any family should. They did not wish to be present at the press conference, knowing that their involvement in helping find their daughters killer would be made public eventually as and when necessary. But for now they were simply a grieving family with grandparents to call with the unbearable news.

DCI Luke Wiley was required to be at the press conference. He was dreading it. Not only was this tremendously upsetting news to deliver, but it was Luke's first press conference after returning to work. It had been agreed that only facts were to be given and nothing about Emma Jones was to be mentioned. The police would reveal this double, falsified identity later only when they felt that they had come to a dead end. The last thing they wanted was for Grace's killer to know that the police understood that the identity of Emma Jones existed. They weren't certain, but it was highly likely that Grace's bag and phone were taken by the killer, either to hide the falsified identity, or simply to discard. Either way, they wanted to find these items or pretend that they didn't know who Emma Jones was.

The press room was on the first floor of the building and Hana and Luke took the lift down together.

'Are you up for this?' Hana asked.

'Honestly, I just want it over with. I wish we weren't having this presser, but we can't withhold the fact that we have found Grace Feist. It's a no-win situation, so the faster it's over and we can get back to work, the better.'

They entered the smaller ancillary room next to the conference room where two way glass formed the small window in the wall between them. The conference room was absolutely packed.

O'Donnell was standing with his arms crossed in the smaller room staring through the glass.

'Stephen,' said Luke.

'Afternoon, Wiley. Ready for this? You've got a full house.'

'I'm surprised there are so many reporters, Sir,' said Hana. 'Do you think there has been another leak?'

O'Donnell glowered at her.

'No,' he sneered. 'There hasn't been a leak. But it has been over two months since we've called one of these. They're curious. And they're about to eat us alive. After you, Wiley.'

He gestured towards the door.

'Senior officers first, Commander,' Luke replied.

'Oh Jesus,' said Hana, as she stepped past them both and opened the door to walk into the conference room. As she did so, the din of the room ceased immediately and a sea of journalists all pulled out their phones, toggled their side buttons to silent and got ready to press 'record'.

Luke and O'Donnell followed her and Luke went to the podium at the front of the room. He shuffled the papers that had been handed to him by a media officer and that he had quickly scanned in the lift. Luke folded the papers in half and lay them down on the podium. There would be no gazing down at this announcement.

'Thank you for assembling at this short notice,' he said.

Luke scanned the room to acquaint himself with who exactly was there. The usual suspects, with Toby Peacock in the front row. This would have to be brief.

'For those of you who are new here, I am Detective Chief Inspector Luke Wiley of the Serious Crime Unit here at Scotland Yard.'

He paused and looked straight ahead. Hana felt the urge to bow her head for what Luke was about to say but she was riveted to Luke's face, waiting for the words to come out of his mouth.

'On Friday morning, a dog walker alerted police that the body of a young woman was in Regent Canal, just south of Broadway Market in Hackney, East London. Officers attended the scene and retrieved the body. DNA tests were pending and they have been received and confirmed today. It is with the deepest regret that we inform you that the identity of the young woman is Grace Feist.'

The wave of sound that cascaded through the conference room — the breaths taken, the oh my gods, and the lack of an instant response of questions indicated that there had been no leak. For every journalist in the room, this news was a shock.

'Jamie, Rosamund and Emily Feist have been informed and they ask that their privacy is respected as they come to terms with this unfathomable loss and grieve together. I would ask that you respect this request. Any questions should not be directed to the family at any time.'

And then the questions came as an avalanche. Every voice wanted to be loudest, desperate to be called on, and for a room of British journalists, very unusually they had all jumped to their feet.

Luke sighed and stepped back from the podium momentarily. He decided to not even bother to call on anyone individually, or to try to hear what was being asked. He simply made up the question he thought he could answer in his head, pretended he had heard it and then spoke into the microphone.

'Yes, we are aware of the six year and one month period of time between Grace's disappearance and her body being found. We do not yet know her whereabouts during this time. Next.'

Luke scanned the room and towards the back he spotted a tall man in jeans, a navy collared shirt and large, rectangular tortoise shell glasses. His arms were at his sides, not holding a phone, and Luke couldn't quite see with the throng of people in front of him, but his hands were probably in their pockets. They usually were.

Luke caught his eye, held the stare for a second longer than would be expected to make sure that his next gesture was interpreted correctly, then he jerked his head slightly up towards the ceiling. The tall man slowly nodded.

'That's a good question, thank you for asking it,' Luke said, fabricating yet another question in his head. 'Grace's family has lots of questions about where Grace has been all of this time and everyone here at Scotland Yard will be working flat out to answer them and bring her killer to justice. Thank you for coming.'

The questions were still echoing down the hall as Luke maneuvered his way out of the conference room and towards the lift to head back to the seventh floor. His mobile phone began to ring and he stopped to answer it.

Nicolson was on the other end of the line. The initial shock felt by the Feist family had led Nicolson to be able to ask some questions that the detectives probably had asked six years ago, but then suspects were found and interrogated and the questions asked of the family faded away. And knowing what they knew now, they had a different significance.

What were Grace's dreams for the future growing up? Did she ever talk about a daydream where she lived somewhere else? What aspirations did she have in terms of a job and a career? Was there anything they could think of that would lead them to discover why Grace didn't simply come home?

But the willingness of the family to consider these possibilities had begun to erode and Rosamund was demanding to be taken to Grace's flat. Luke said that he and Hana would meet them there.

When Luke stepped out of the lift at the seventh floor, the tall man with the tortoiseshell glasses was standing at the security desk. Rowdy was talking to him.

'Laura won't let me through,' he said. 'I did tell her that I'd been summoned by the famous flick of DCI Wiley's head.'

'Hello Henry,' said Luke, extending his hand.

'Luke,' Henry shook it warmly.

'He was flirting with me and I was enjoying it,' Rowdy said. 'Now you've killed it. Thanks a lot.'

Luke swiped his card over the security reader and held the barrier open for Henry to walk through.

'Don't you have to sign me in?'

'Consider this a social visit.'

'Or,' said Henry, 'You'd rather not have me here officially?'

Luke smiled but said nothing and ushered Henry into his office. It had been a good year and a half since Luke had seen Henry MacAskill and his hair was a little bit greyer around the temples. Henry was one of the only journalists Luke trusted. He was always respectful, wrote thoughtfully about police work and when he was told that he couldn't print something, he never did. Luke and Henry could be known to sink a few beers after work when the occasion arose and while they weren't exactly friends, they would both scratch each others' backs and not mind doing so. Luke liked him and for a journalist, that was saying a lot.

'When are you going to ask Rowdy out?'

'Luke, she's probably a decade older than me.'

'So?'

Henry laughed.

'It's good to see you. When I heard you had returned to the Met I thought the person who told me was joking. I had imagined you sailing around the Mediterranean on a yacht.'

Luke didn't take well to this kind of teasing from many people, but with Henry it was allowed.

'Thanks for coming upstairs, Henry.'

'Of course. And really Luke. It's good to see you. I know it must still be a rotten time.'

The fact that Henry had led with this small condolence instead of leading with a barrage of questions about Grace Feist was the confirmation that Luke needed to ask what he was about to ask.

'I need something from you. Very, very discreetly.'

'Shoot.'

'I'm going to guess that you, or one of your colleagues, has had the need at some point to open a bank account with falsified documents. I need to know how I would go about doing that if I was eighteen years old.'

'You have more than you said in the conference.'

'Yes.'

'Okay, as soon as I know, you'll know.'

'Thank you, Henry.'

Henry stretched out his long legs and then stood up to leave. He paused at the door, his hand on the door handle.

'You used to have a photo of Sadie on your desk.'

Sometimes Luke thought that Henry would have made a better detective than a journalist.

'Good memory,' Luke said.

'Don't bring it back,' Henry suddenly said. 'She doesn't belong here.'

Henry looked at Luke and Luke tried to figure out what he was saying. And then Henry was gone.

# TWENTY

When Hana and Luke arrived at the flat by Broadway Market, Nicolson was sitting in an unmarked police van that she had somehow commandeered with all three remaining members of the Feist family. Jamie's wheelchair was in the back of the van.

Luke knocked on the window and Nicolson lowered it.

'All okay?' he asked.

'We just need a minute. I think we are taking it all in.'

Luke told them to take their time and headed to the front door. Rachel Champion had already been called and was waiting inside. She opened the door before Luke reached it and Hana took this as her cue to join them, hurrying inside.

'Do you know if Nick is home?' Luke pointed to the inner door on the ground level.

Rachel shook her head.

'No, he hasn't been here for a couple of days. And my other flat mate is still away.'

'Okay, great. Let's head upstairs.'

'I saw it on the news. I mean, it's everywhere. Emma was

Grace Feist, wasn't she?' Rachel blurted out, before they had even moved to head up the stairs to the flat.

'I'm afraid so,' said Hana. 'Come on, let's make a cup of tea and talk upstairs.'

When they were settled in the tiny sitting room once again, Rachel's first question was completely understandable.

'Am I in danger here? Did Emma, I mean Grace, escape from her kidnapper and he found her and then killed her? Did he know she was living here?'

'We just don't know if Grace's kidnapper was involved in her death. It's very possible that these things are unrelated. We do not believe that you are in any danger being here, but we can find you other accommodation for the next week if you would prefer that,' said Luke.

Rachel nodded and Hana stood up with her mobile and stepped into the stairwell to make the arrangements through the station.

'We are going to have many more questions for you now, Rachel. But that can wait until tomorrow. Now that we know Emma Jones was a fabrication, we're going to need to understand as much of the picture you can paint us about how Grace arrived here and what happened in those first few days and weeks, okay?

Rachel nodded once more.

'There's one more thing I thought of.'

The hairs on the back of Luke's neck involuntarily stood up. He realized at this point that they had so little to go on that he was relying on this terrified young woman who through no fault of her own had become caught up in something so much bigger than her.

'What's that?'

'When Emma, sorry, I mean Grace turned up to properly move in, she didn't have anything with her. The room came furnished, but she still only had one duffel bag with her. I remember asking her if her family was dropping off suitcases and other stuff later and she said they were, but I don't think that ever happened.'

'Do you know how she found out about the vacancy here?'

'We posted the listing online. But I know that she said someone from the community centre where she worked saw the listing first.'

'So Grace was already working there?' Luke asked.

'I think so. But she was staying at a hotel.'

'How do you know that?'

'She had the little shampoos. You know the miniature bottles you get in hotel bathrooms? She had taken them all. I do that too.'

Luke was suddenly standing.

'Do you know what hotel it was?'

'No idea,' said Rachel. 'But I bet we still have one in the bathroom. I can check?'

Hana walked back into the sitting room and asked Luke what he was saying. He realized that he was whispering under his breath to himself. *Please have it. Please have it.*

Rachel had it. She emerged from the bathroom holding a small cream bottle with a silver cap.

'It's the moisturizer. These never get used up.'

Luke took it from her and studied the front of the bottle. It was from a Travel Inn, of which there must be a dozen in London alone. But it was a start.

'Thank you, Rachel. This is extremely helpful. Hana will get you sorted for tonight, but in the meantime, we have Grace's family outside and they would like to see Grace's room. I hope you understand.'

'Oh, sure,' Rachel said. 'Do I have to see them? I mean, I'm happy to. But...just maybe not now?'

'I think that's probably best for everyone at the moment.

Lots of time for that. Shall we get some things together for you and head outside? You're all set for tonight and Officer Parker is on his way to collect you.'

———

Luke and Officer Parker had carried Jamie Feist up the stairs. He asked to be seated on Grace's bed.

Emily sat next to her father and Rosamund paced the tiny room, back and forth, staring at every single thing in it.

If ever there was a broken man, it was Jamie Feist sitting on his dead daughter's bed in a strange room that her family had never seen, stroking her pillow. He wept silently.

It was Emily who spoke first.

'I thought maybe it would smell like her. But it doesn't smell like Grace in here.'

'Does anything seem familiar to you in here?' Luke asked.

Rosamund's arms flung up in the air in response to Luke's question.

'This doesn't make sense,' she said. 'Why the hell was she here? If she was released from her kidnapper, why didn't she come home? Grace knew we would never leave there, we would never abandon her.'

Rosamund began to weep as well, her hands gripping her arms so hard that her skin began to show white marks where her fingers had dug into the flesh.

Hana couldn't imagine anything worse than this. A twelve year old girl had been abducted and then released years later, but did not go home to her family, only to be murdered shortly afterwards. How could the Feists live with this?

'There must be a reason she was here. Detective Wiley, there has to be a reason,' Rosamund pleaded.

There must have been a small part of Jamie and Rosamund Feist that had already said goodbye to their daughter. As much as they hoped and prayed that she would be returned home safely, after six long years there must have been a sense of the inevitable. And now, right in front of them, was the unthinkable. That Grace had been set free and chose to not come home. Luke and Hana understood that in this moment, the reason for this was more important to the family than finding the person who killed their daughter. This wound was greater.

# TWENTY-ONE

D r. Nicky Bowman was loading her dishwasher at ten o'clock that evening. The television was on in the background at the other end of the ground floor where two steps led down into a sunken living room.

The headline news being read out by the newscaster stopped her momentarily and she listened intently to what was being said.

Grace Feist had been found. She was dead.

It was a shocking headline.

How terribly sad, she thought as she remembered Grace's parents and their appeals on camera six years ago to anyone who may have information that would help bring their daughter home. What they must be feeling today.

The next voice Nicky heard made her stop again. She was confused in the way that one is when they see someone in front of them that they weren't expecting to see in a location where that person generally isn't found. Except it was the voice of her patient that had startled her in this way.

Nicky grabbed a tea towel and rushed towards the television. Staring back at her was Luke.

She had never seen him in a suit before. How formal his voice sounded without the lilt of grief often peppered with humour. But it was Luke.

The brief coverage of the police press conference ended and the camera moved to the canal where Grace's body had been found, now cleared of police tape and busy with joggers and dog walkers. She wondered if Luke had been standing right there when Grace was pulled out of the water. She understood the huge significance of what this would be like for him.

She had an overwhelming urge to do something that she never did between sessions. She wanted to call her patient.

Nicky thought about her patients often in days of the week between seeing them. This was part of the process — how she reflected on their conversations, what images and thoughts occurred to her later, how she might incorporate them into the next session.

But this was different.

She felt the palpable desire to see Luke, to make sure that he was alright.

Nicky looked at her phone sitting on the kitchen counter where she had left it. Calling a patient in between sessions wasn't entirely appropriate.

But she could text.

———

Luke had been lying in bed, completely exhausted from the day's events. Every single hour had been emotionally charged and he had driven to Sussex and back. But when he crawled under the duvet and stretched his legs out on the bamboo sheets, he knew he would struggle to sleep.

He missed his wife.

When cases were hard like this — and one hadn't been this

hard in a very long time — Luke would come home to Sadie and a small part of his working brain was able to switch off. It is impossible to not feel changed, even in the span of a day, by someone you love caring for you. It is a balm, and a reassurance, and the ability to know that you are not alone.

At a quarter past ten, his bedside light already off, but Luke was still wide awake, his phone screen burst to life and the chime of a text echoed through the bedroom. He knew he would not sleep with his phone on silent some time now with the discovery of Grace Feist's body.

Without sitting up, Luke reached over and tilted the screen so he could see the name on it.

Nicky Bowman.

Luke opened the screen to read the text.

**I just saw the news. I'm here tomorrow if you want to see me.**

A small flutter of relief glowed through Luke's body. He sank into his pillow.

What he didn't know was that Nicky was still holding the phone, wondering if the typing bubble would appear. Was Luke still working? Did he mind her texting?

The bubble appeared almost immediately.

**Thanks for your msg. I should be at work for 7am and it will be a long day.**

And that's how Luke found himself sitting in Nicky's office at six o'clock the next morning.

It was still dark and the lamps were all on in the room, their soft light making it feel warmer than it was on a cold November morning. Two strong Americanos were already sitting on the table between them next to the tissue box when Luke came into the room.

'If I remember correctly you like it strong and no milk.'

'Thank you,' said Luke. 'I really appreciate you meeting with me so early.'

Nicky nodded and paused before she spoke.

'I'm glad that it worked out.'

Any observer would have thought that this was an imposition for Nicky, her demeanour quiet and reserved. They would not have seen the relief she felt to have Luke here so early in her day.

'We don't really talk about my cases. Specifically. I mean, there hasn't been the need to do so because I've been sitting at my desk since I've been back at work.'

'We talked about the Marcus and Venetia Wright case,' Nicky reminded him.

'Yes,' said Luke, considering his answer. 'Except that was in the past, it had already happened. Grace is very much in the present.'

Nicky felt herself freeze slightly at the mention of Grace's name. She needed to remind herself that her role was to help and support Luke, not to figure out what had happened to Grace Feist.

'How have the last few days been for you?'

'Do you mean was I there when we pulled a dead woman out of the water?'

'Yes,' said Nicky. 'Amongst the many things I mean, that is one of them.'

'Hana was there, too. I'm okay. It felt like just part of the job, or at least it did at the time.'

'And now?' asked Nicky.

Luke thought for a moment, gathering his thoughts, not wanting to waste time when he would need to get up and go in about half an hour's time.

'Okay, Nicky. I'm going to make an assumption here that I need you to run with. Since you are the therapist overseeing my reintegration back into work...' Luke looked at her before continuing. '...apparently. Then I feel I can discuss aspects of Grace's disappearance and murder with you.'

Nicky swallowed and gave Luke the space to keep talking.

'I have a question for you. Strictly speaking as a therapist, what could possibly be the reasons that a girl who is kidnapped at age twelve and then seemingly released under her own free will at age eighteen, would not run straight to the police or back to her parents?'

The sound that came through Nicky's pursed lips as she slowly exhaled was soft and low. What she wanted to say was, *Jesus*. But she took a moment to think.

'Two primary reasons, off the top of my head.'

'Okay,' said Luke. 'What are they, in no particular order.'

'She could have felt empathy towards her kidnapper.'

Luke chortled.

'Come on,' he said. 'You mean Stockholm syndrome?'

'Well,' Nicky said, taking a sip of her Americano, 'the term "Stockholm Syndrome" has been sensationalized a bit. This process that sometimes happens — although it is extremely rare — is a trauma response. In order to preserve yourself, in order to survive, you begin to view the person who has taken you but not killed you as the person who is now actually keeping you alive. And the victim can begin to feel emotions that you and I would otherwise find bizarre.'

Luke considered what his therapist was saying and tried to get his head around it.

'And the second reason?'

'That's a little bit simpler. There is a serious and grave imminent threat to life.'

# TWENTY-TWO

Luke kept his conversation with Nicky to himself when he arrived back at the Incident Room. The board was covered in more detail about Emma Jones and Grace Feist — each in their own column for now — and there was palpable excitement in the room.

'What's up?' Luke asked Hana, who was leaning over an open file folder on the table, scrutinizing it.

'Morning,' she said. 'Rowdy to the rescue. We have details on the three separate payments that came into Emma Jones' bank account. They were always in the same amount — £50 — so it looks like payment for services, maybe? Two of the addresses are close to where she was living and one a little closer into town.

Luke didn't bother to take off his jacket, but picked up a large blueberry muffin that sat in a box of pastries on the table and bit into it without taking off the wrapper.

'Sharma,' he said, after he had swallowed. 'Any luck with the neighbour's laptop?'

'It's taking a little while, Sir,' he replied. 'Tech guys...they always wipe their browser history. I'll get it, but it's a bit time consuming. He knows what he's doing.'

'Bet you know more, Sharma.'

Hana raised her eyebrows at her partner, who had eaten the entire muffin in under a minute.

'Why so interested in the neighbour's laptop? We don't think this is our guy.'

'He's not *not* our guy for the time being,' Luke said. 'And I'm still curious about the laptop. We didn't find one in Grace's room. If she was spending time with Nick Tuft, then maybe she used his.'

'I'm on it, Sir,' Sharma confirmed again.

'Any sign of Philippa this morning?' Luke asked the room, addressing no one in particular.

There was a mumbled *no* from the room and Luke and Hana headed out the door.

———

Knocking on the door of the first address received by First National Bank, Luke and Hana stood back and waited. It was eventually opened by a woman in her forties, flustered, on a phone call and looking confused at the two people standing on her doorstep.

'Sorry,' she said into the phone. 'One second.'

The woman lowered her mobile.

Hana introduced herself and Luke and explained the reason for their visit. The woman hung up her call and said that she did know Emma Jones.

'She tutors my daughter in French.'

If the woman took in the look of surprise on the detectives' faces, she didn't let on.

'I'm sorry, what is this about?' she asked.

'Do you have five minutes? It might be easier to explain

inside,' Hana said. But at this point Luke and Hana didn't really know what they were going to explain. How quickly would this news story get out of control — if it wasn't already — if they revealed to this woman that Emma Jones was actually Grace Feist? Who would she tell? Would she recognize Luke from the news the previous evening?

But what Luke and Hana encountered was a woman who was exhausted by her life. She was juggling her kids, their lives, her job, and probably her husband. The woman did not seem particularly phased by their line of questioning and revealed that "Emma" had been tutoring her ten year old daughter in French in preparation for her school entrance exam and had been doing so weekly for five weeks. The woman had seen an ad for "Emma's" services on the noticeboard in the community centre. She was fantastic, her daughter loved her, and the woman had recommended her to a couple of other parents at her daughter's school.

'But why are you asking all of this?'

There aren't many times in a career that a detective should lie, but this was one of them. To delay the inevitable they told her that there had been a discrepancy in something financial and they were assisting Emma with this. That she would not be attending the tutoring session next week, but that Luke or Hana would be in touch to follow up as quickly as possible. They left their cards and the woman seemed grateful to show them out and get on with the frenzy of her day.

The phone numbers of the other two parents in hand, Hana made the calls as they drove back to Scotland Yard. Both confirmed the exact same details. Somehow in the six years she was missing, Grace Feist had learned to speak French.

Hana added this detail to the board in the Incident Room when the detectives returned.

Philippa Nicolson had joined the team and you could tell that the more junior members were thrilled to have her there. She had been on the phone when Luke and Hana walked in and now looked up at what Hana had written.

'You're kidding me,' Nicolson said.

'I know,' said Luke. 'What the hell do you make of this?'

She was baffled. When Grace Feist went missing she did not speak French. She wasn't even taking it at school any longer.

'Her kidnapper was French,' Hana said. 'Or at least spoke French.'

'Or,' said Sharma, 'she was taken to France six years ago.'

'Unlikely,' said Luke. 'Borders were tight when Grace was abducted — she wouldn't have gotten out of the country easily. And Interpol was all over this, too. If she had turned up in some classroom in the French countryside, we would have known about it.'

'Maybe she had some sort of access to one of those online French classes. You know, that you go through yourself with audio lessons.'

'If she was online, then she would have made contact,' said Nicolson.

Luke was quiet when she said this, unsure of what to think.

'Have we gotten any further with the Travel Inns?' he asked to no one in particular. 'How many are there in London?'

A voice from the back of the room spoke up. It was a quiet, studious woman in her early 30s called Joy Lombardi.

'There are 75 Travel Inns in London, Sir,' she said. 'And that's not counting the outer boroughs. But we are calling all of them to see if Grace stayed there in the weeks preceding her move-in date to Rachel's flat. We're starting with hotel locations close to there and moving outwards. So far we're on hotel number twenty eight.'

'Good work, Lombardi,' said Nicolson, speaking for everyone in the room at such a tedious task.

'Is there anything else we're missing, apart from the obvious?' Luke said.

A soft rap of knuckles on the open door made every head in the Incident Room swivel towards it.

It was Rowdy.

'Emily Feist is downstairs. She wants to see you.'

The look between Nicolson, Luke and Hana was brief before the three detectives stood up and moved towards the door.

'My office, please, Rowdy,' said Luke.

'No,' said Nicolson. 'Let go outside to meet her. We're used to it up here, but I don't want to frighten her.'

'Agreed,' said Hana.

Downstairs in the reception area of Scotland Yard stood Emily Feist. She didn't look frightened at all. As the detectives approached her, she strode over to them.

'You have to come back to Grace's flat,' Emily said. 'There's something you need to see.'

# Twenty-Three

Hana knew it. Sisters have their own set of rules, their own unique relationship.

The flat was empty when they arrived back at it and the detectives let Emily lead the way upstairs and into Grace's room. In the car, Emily had said that she wasn't sure what she was looking for, but that she had to try to find answers. No one asked her anything further, all three detectives too curious to do anything but let the search take place in real time as they watched.

Emily entered the bedroom and took a good look around. She walked over to the bedside table and reached her hand underneath the top section that held the table's solitary drawer. She bent down to look at the underside of the drawer — space meant for piling books or other sundries, but in Grace's sparsely filled room, there was nothing in it.

Emily then pulled out the drawer, which had already been emptied of its contents and taken to the lab at Scotland Yard. There hadn't been much in it, an old magazine, some hair elastics, lip balm. She pulled the drawer all of the way out and removed it from the table, then flipped it over. She sat down on the floor as she did this, and sighed.

'I thought...' she said, and then she stopped.

Standing up, Emily picked up the entire table, now much lighter with the drawer removed and turned it upside down.

Hana involuntarily gasped.

'I knew it,' Emily said and moved her hand towards the table.

'Stop!' Luke said.

Emily froze in mid-movement and turned to look at him.

'I don't have any,' he said, patting his jacket pockets.

'I do,' Hana said, pulling a pair of latex gloves out of her own.

All four of them stared at what was in front of them. A plastic sandwich bag, closed with its connecting tabs at the top was affixed to the bottom of the table with two strips of gaffer tape.

Hana carefully pulled the bag away from the underside the table, being careful not to rip the plastic. Inside the bag looked like a folded piece of paper.

'Emily,' said Nicolson. 'How did you know this would be here?'

It was at this point that Emily, who had been so calm and determined since announcing her arrival at Scotland Yard, began to fall apart.

'I'm sorry,' she sniffed as the tears began to form. 'I'm so sorry, I didn't say anything back then. I...'

'It's okay,' said Luke. 'It doesn't matter. Can you just explain to us now?'

Emily sat down on her sister's bed and for the first time that day, looked like a sixteen year old, tucking her knees underneath her chin and clasping her arms around legs.

'It was all crazy when Grace went missing. There were police officers everywhere and you were there,' she nodded and

Luke and Nicolson. 'I didn't remember until later and I just looked myself. My sister used to hide things in a plastic bag with tape like this underneath the drawer in her bedside table. She didn't know that I knew, but I saw her. I used to sneak into her bedroom when she wasn't home and look inside it.'

'What was inside it?' Hana asked.

Emily swallowed and continued to tell the detectives what she hadn't said for the past six years.

'Usually it was just stupid stuff like notes from friends that you pass in class. Stuff like that.'

'But why did she keep things like this hidden? What was the point?' asked Luke.

Both Nicolson and Hana looked at him with raised eyebrows.

'You weren't ever a teenage girl,' said Nicolson.

Luke shrugged his shoulders and motioned for Emily to continue.

'It was a few weeks after she went missing and I checked to see if the bag was still there. It was. All that was in it was a pack of cigarettes, but it was mostly empty. There were just two left. I'm sorry I didn't say anything. I don't know why she had them and I didn't want her to get into trouble. I kept thinking that she was away somewhere and going to come back and then would really be in huge trouble. I didn't want to make it worse.'

'It's okay,' said Nicolson.

Whether or not this was the truth didn't really matter anymore. Could they have tested the cigarette package for DNA that may have led them to Grace's kidnapper? It was a possibility. But there was no point making Emily suffer for a decision that a frightened ten year old girl had made six years earlier. A girl who was now a teenager grieving the death of the sister she had now lost twice.

They all looked at the bag and Hana slowly opened it, pulling out its contents.

There were two folded pieces of paper. One looked like a piece of printer paper, bright white and folded neatly into quarters. The other was a lined piece of off-white paper that looked like it had been torn off a pad, also folded into quarters.

Which one to open first, the three detectives were all thinking.

Hana picked up the lined piece and eased it flat, holding the corners with her fingertips.

It was a list of some kind, and handwritten.

'Is this Grace's handwriting?' Hana asked Emily.

The girl looked at the sheet of paper and studied it.

'Maybe? It kind of looks like hers, but I'm not sure.'

The list had ten or so names and places on it. They all descended in a neat column.

'These are names of churches,' said Luke. 'And sometimes a street name next to it.'

'Emily, does your family go to church?' Hana asked.

Luke and Nicolson already knew the answer to this. They didn't — or at least they didn't six years ago. The Feists were not a religious family.

Emily confirmed that this was still the case and the detectives looked baffled. Something made Hana hesitate before opening the second folded piece of paper. She looked at Luke for guidance and he nodded. She slowly unfurled the sheet and they couldn't believe what they were looking at. Luke, Nicolson and Hana turned to stare at Emily who was, in turn, openmouthed at the image on the paper in Hana's hands.

It was Emily. Sixteen year old Emily Feist was staring back at her.

# TWENTY-FOUR

The original pieces of paper taken from underneath Grace Feist's table went to the lab for processing and scanned copies were stuck to the board in the Incident Room. Hana didn't like how the board was rapidly filling up and all that they had were more questions.

The debate raged briefly between members of the team on the seventh floor of Scotland Yard. Did Grace take the photograph of Emily, or had she somehow otherwise acquired it?

Sharma pointed to the board where they had details taken from Rachel Champion about Emma Jones.

'Rachel said that she had a mobile phone. We just haven't found it. So if Grace was looking for Emily, saw her and snapped a photo on her phone, she would have it on there.'

'Or she did that,' said Luke, 'and then printed the photo out and hid it before deleting the one on her phone in case someone scrolled through it and Grace didn't want it to be seen by anyone else.'

'Maybe,' said Sharma. 'Except, Sir, no one under the age of thirty owns a printer.'

'That's true, Sir,' said Lombardi, from the back of the room.

Nicolson had been unusually quiet since they dropped Emily Feist back at home, reassuring her the entire way there, and returning to Scotland Yard. Luke knew from experience that this was probably a good sign.

'Philippa?'

Nicolson sighed and rubbed her eyes with the heels of her palms. She stood up and walked to the front of the Incident Room and leaned against the table that held paper cups and a box of chocolates, only the coconut ones remaining — obviously everyone's least favourite.

'Let's start again. We have two items and they indicate two different things. The photograph of Emily is hidden...why? Because Grace couldn't risk someone seeing it and figuring out that they were sisters. Grace was terrified of her true identity being revealed. And the list of churches seems to point to Grace searching for something. Otherwise, why list them and keep the list hidden? She was searching for something that she didn't want anyone to know she was looking for. What does this all say to you, Luke?'

Luke paused and considered what Nicolson had just said. He tried to link the two hidden items, as if doing so could give them the vital clue they needed to find Grace's killer. Or kidnapper. Or both.

'You only hide something if there is a threat to you should it be found,' he said.

'If Emily didn't take this photograph of her sister,' Hana said, 'then who did?'

'And how did Grace get ahold of it?' answered Luke.

'Too many questions,' said Nicolson. 'Let's start again. Think of the basics.'

Luke couldn't help but smile and the rest of the room

probably wondered what on earth he was smiling about. But in this moment he realized that there was a part of him that had missed Philippa Nicolson. How much she had taught him in the brief year they worked together. This was a phrase that she said too many times for Luke to count.

*Let's start again. Think of the basics.*

It was good advice. And they needed it. He looked over at Hana and his quiet delight at his old partner had been caught by her. She looked at the floor.

Nicolson explained that they needed to stop looking back at when Grace was abducted six years ago and similarly, to stop focusing on two months earlier when she had moved into Rachel's flat.

'The how's and why's of these things are too big right now. But we have something closer to us and we need to focus on that,' she said.

'Her murder,' Sharma said.

'Exactly. What happened three days ago? Where was she? I want to re-canvas the area around Rachel's flat,' Nicolson paused. 'But I also want to canvas the street that the Feists live on.'

'Why?' asked Lombardi.

'Back to basics. It's where Grace is from and if we can eliminate it, then great. But I wonder if there is something there.'

'I'll go,' volunteered Hana.

Luke looked up and her and smiled.

'Why don't you take Officer Parker with you?' he said. 'Where is Parker?'

'He was sent back to his station, Sir,' said Sharma. 'Which is a shame, because he was the one who brought in the pastries.'

'Well, then we'd better get him back here,' said Luke.

———

Officer Parker was thrilled to be walking the streets of Muswell Hill in the north end of London with DS Sawatsky. It would have been years before he could dream of being promoted to this kind of work. Hana had been irritated at Luke's suggestion that Parker tag along. She didn't want to be babysitting some junior officer and she really didn't want to look like she couldn't handle this assignment herself in front of Nicolson.

But at least Parker wasn't chatty. There was nothing worse that someone who was chatty in these situations.

Hana and Parker were taking a very good look around. They knocked on every door and asked about anyone new in the area, anything suspicious, had they seen a young woman that could have been Grace Feist? Everyone they spoke to stopped what they were doing and engaged meaningfully with them. Grace's death had sent shockwaves through this neighbourhood just as her disappearance had six years earlier. Everyone wanted to help.

'May I ask,' said Parker, as they walked between the homes, 'what you think may have happened to Grace? Do you think that her disappearance and her death are connected?'

'I do,' Hana said. 'I have the feeling that everyone in the Incident Room is thinking the same thing. We just can't prove it yet. But it would be one mighty unfortunate coincidence should they not be connected somehow.'

'No family should go through this,' Parker said quietly.

'No,' said Hana. 'They shouldn't.'

The houses on the Feists street were close together, even though they were all detached. They were small homes with the biggest asset at the back in the form of large gardens. As Hana looked around she thought that it would have been a pleasant place to grow up.

'Ah,' she said, touching Parker's arm, which both of them were slightly startled by.

'What?'

'There,' she pointed to the small camera above the door-bell on a house across the street from the Feists and one house to the left.

'I've been looking for a doorbell camera or any other kind of home alarm CCTV and this is the first one I've seen,' Hana said.

Ringing the doorbell and staring into the camera, Hana and Parker waited.

The door was answered by a woman in her sixties and like everyone else on the street, she was happy to speak to them.

'My neighbour actually rang already and said that you two were on the street. I wonder if the camera on my door may be of use to you?'

'Those were our thoughts exactly,' said Hana. 'Thanks.'

Hana and Parker were invited inside and shown into the sitting room.

'I just need to get my mobile phone,' the woman said. 'It's very clever. If there is any movement then the camera begins to record and I get an alert on my phone. I have the sound switched off because there are quite a few alerts in the day. Because I'm so close to the pavement, anyone walking by will activate the camera. But it's a quiet street, so it's not too bad.'

When the woman returned, she showed Parker and Hana how the system worked and they scrolled back to the date of Grace's murder. The footage was quite clear for such a small device and they could quickly see in the camera's alerts that day that nothing looked out of the ordinary.

'We'd like to go through this footage at the station,' Hana said. 'Is there a way that we can do that?'

'I'm not sure,' the woman said. 'There may be a way to

view it online, but I'm afraid I'm not that tech savvy and only look at what pops up on my phone. And I can't have you take away my phone.'

'Of course. We'll figure something out. Thank you for your time and we will get our tech colleague to pop around later today and see what he can manage. His name is...'

'DS Sawatsky,' Parker interrupted.

Hana was surprised to have been cut off by this junior officer and turned to glare at him when Parker shoved the woman's mobile in front of her.

'Look,' he said.

Parker had scrolled back to three days before Grace was found in the canal and clicked on a camera activation at 11:02am. And there, plain as day, was Grace Feist.

Grace's back was to the camera as she was staring at the house in which she used to live. And then she turned quickly behind her, as if to see if anyone was watching her. She looked almost directly into the camera.

Hana suddenly felt very cold and her fingertips were tingling slightly.

'Do you know if any of your neighbours have a similar camera installed?' Hana asked.

'No,' the woman replied. 'I don't think so and I always thought it strange that no one else took up the offer.'

Hana leaned forward in her chair and could feel Officer Parker do the same.

'What offer?'

'The camera company. They had a representative in the neighbourhood and it was a great deal. The camera equipment and installation was completely free. All I had to do was keep it for a minimum of one year while they performed external checks on it for functionality or something. It's a brand new product that they are testing and I just thought, why not? I get security for free and I couldn't care less what the company is doing.'

Hana was now standing up.

'When did this company install the camera?'

'Let me think,' the woman said. 'It must have been a little over two months ago.'

# TWENTY-FIVE

Nicolson had valiantly fought her way to the front of the queue at the bar and was doing her best not to spill the drinks on her way back to the table. The pub was heaving and Hana had dashed to a small table for two in the corner when she saw a couple get up to leave.

'Thanks,' she said, as Nicolson placed a double gin and tonic in front of her.

Nicolson placed her own large glass of white wine down and removed her coat, tossing it onto the windowsill next to them.

'Was this one of your usual spots?' Hana asked her.

'It was,' Nicolson replied. 'I haven't missed it one bit.'

Hana chuckled.

'I bet. Your home is lovely.'

'Thank you,' Nicolson said, taking more of a gulp than a sip of her wine.

Hana wasn't entirely sure why Philippa Nicolson had invited her for a drink at the end of the day. The afternoon had been manic after Hana and Parker called into the Incident Room with the report of the camera footage. Parker had remained with the Feists' bewildered neighbour, waiting for Sharma and other support to arrive while Hana had returned to Scotland Yard.

It had been a relief to crack the case open, even just a little bit.

'So,' Hana began, wondering what on earth she was doing there. 'What do you think the camera footage really shows us? That Grace was really about to go home?'

Nicolson waved off her suggestion, her hand whipping through the air and the other one on her wine glass. Hana suddenly felt silly and inferior and wished that she wasn't sitting there.

'Take a break, Sawatsky. We are all going to need clear heads.'

Hana looked at her rather large gin and tonic and wondered about that.

'How do you find working with Wiley?' Nicolson suddenly asked.

'Oh. It's good. We get on well. Always have done. It's been good to have him back at work. I was in between partners when he left and I don't think O'Donnell knew what to do with me.'

Nicolson smiled at her.

'He's still such a prick.'

Hana burst out laughing and raised her glass. Nicolson raised hers and they clinked them together.

'I don't like working with people I don't know. Who I don't yet trust,' Nicolson said.

'Is that the point of this drink then, Ma'am?' Hana shot back.

Nicolson leaned back in her chair and surveyed the younger woman sitting across from her. The woman who reminded her of herself, twenty five years earlier.

What Hana didn't know is that Nicolson trusted her

immediately. She knew Luke well enough to understand that it was his estimation of her that Nicolson valued. And she had discretely asked around. She had been told of Hana's unwavering dedication to Luke over the past year and a half. The fall out from the Marcus Wright case and then through Sadie's death. Where some of their colleagues were a tad on the pejorative side in their analysis of Luke and Hana's relationship, expressing disdain at some of the details — Hana picking up Luke in the morning, their shared love of yoga, how close she was to his wife — Nicolson saw these qualities as the mark of an empathetic person and subsequently, an excellent detective.

What Nicolson hadn't been able to determine was what made Hana tick. She had asked Rowdy to slip her Hana's personnel file and it didn't reveal much. Interestingly, Hana was ex-military, which you didn't see very often at detective rank. And not only that, she had been in special forces training which was, again, unusual for a woman.

'This isn't a cloak and daggers exercise, DS Sawatsky. I'm much more straightforward than that.'

'Your reputation does precede you,' said Hana. 'So exactly why did you want to have a drink?'

'There are a few reasons,' Nicolson admitted. 'I'd like to know how Luke is getting on. It's been a terrible time for him and I know that you have been instrumental in helping him through it and seeing him back into the Met. And, of course, I understand that you were close to Sadie.'

'I was.'

'And how are you?' Nicolson asked.

'I don't know how to answer that. I miss her. I think about her most hours of the day. I'm trying to find a way to make my grief fit into my life. And then I think about Luke and how much worse this is for him in a way that I can't possibly begin to understand and so I just get on with it.'

'And Luke?'

'He's doing as well as possible, I think. Sometimes I feel like I push him too hard and I stop asking him about it. I think we both find that a bit easier at the moment.'

'Do you think he feels he made the right decision to come back to work?'

'You'd have to ask Luke that, Ma'am.'

'And do you think you made the right decision to leave the special forces and join the Met?'

Hana was so taken aback by the question that she was uncharacteristically dumbfounded.

'I had Rowdy pull your file for me,' Nicolson said. 'I may as well tell you now. Rowdy is a master of keeping secrets but I can see that she respects you, so she was bound to tell you eventually.'

Hana begrudgingly was impressed by the chutzpah of this woman sitting in front of her. Once a detective, always a detective.

'Yes, I was in the forces for eight years.'

'But you joined after university. That's not a usual career path.'

'I don't sit still for very long.'

'What made you leave the forces? That file I haven't been able to pull yet — it's a little higher than even my last rank.'

Hana wanted to tell Philippa Nicolson what had happened. And in that moment she also understood how effective Nicolson had been as a senior detective. She barely knew the woman and was about to open up a wound that she had spent many years trying to bury. She had thrown herself into her work, she had kept busy. She had Luke and she used to have Sadie.

As Hana opened her mouth to reply, her phone, sitting on the tabletop lit up and began to buzz. The screen said Luke Wiley.

Hana went to pick it up when Nicolson's phone did the same. Her screen simply said Rowdy.

The two women looked up at each other and both grabbed their phones to answer them. The person on the other end said the exact same thing to each of them.

'You need to come back. Sharma has found something.'

# TWENTY-SIX

It had begun to pour with rain while Nicolson and Hana had been in the pub. Neither woman had an umbrella with them and even though the pub was only two blocks away, they were both soaked to the bone by the time they got back to Scotland Yard.

They knew that whatever had been found was important because Laura Rowdy was in the Incident Room with them instead of in her own office or flitting about the seventh floor dealing with various colleagues requiring a multitude of different pieces of information. And more than that, Laura Rowdy was sitting down.

Luke was not. He was pacing up and down, which didn't get him very far in the small room. Hana flicked her eyes towards the board and scanned it. She didn't see anything new.

'Close the door,' Luke instructed and Nicolson, not at all bothered by this lack of respect for her former rank, shut it softly behind her.

Hana didn't dare take off her jacket, which was dripping onto the floor. She wiped the droplets still lingering on her forehead and wiped her hands on her thighs.

'Sharma,' said Luke. 'Please explain.'

Sharma looked nervous and exhilarated at the same time. His voice broke a bit as he stood up and began speaking.

'It has taken awhile to get into Nick Tuft's laptop. The data either wiped or mostly encrypted. But I've run my sort of own, bespoke, software through his laptop and the internet search history for the last week has finally downloaded.'

'Except,' said Luke, gesturing for him to continue and nodding along, encouraging him to explain the information in the correct order. Hana had seen Luke do this a thousand times.

'Except,' said Sharma, smiling shyly, 'I get a bit bored when this kind of software takes so long to get results. So I started doing some of my own searches. I thought that maybe it would help. And I found something.'

The entire room was silent. Even those members of the team who had been in the room earlier while Hana and Nicolson had been at the pub seemed to be holding their breath. And they already knew what Sharma was about to say.

'Grace's disappearance was unusual in that a body was never found. Until, of course, a few days ago. So I ran a search for five years before her disappearance and five years afterward to see if there were any other girls who went missing and were never found. There couldn't be that many of them and I thought that maybe there would be something about one of these other cases that may give us a clue.'

'How many were there?' asked Hana.

'There were only eight cases.'

Luke had, at this point, lifted his arms up and clasped his hands together, laying them on top of his head. Nicolson and Hana were staring at Bobby Sharma.

'When I pulled the list of eight names up, one jumped out. A girl went missing from north London and to this day hasn't been found. Her name is Caitlin Black.'

Caitlin.

'When did she go missing?' asked Hana.

'Two years before Grace Feist. And she was also twelve years old at the time.'

'Which makes her...' Hana said, before Nicolson interrupted her.

'Two years older than Grace. The older sister that Grace's flatmate told us about.'

# TWENTY-SEVEN

The room wasn't as small as she thought it was at first. Once her eyes had adjusted to the soft glow of light coming from a solitary standing lamp in the corner of the room she could see that it was probably just slightly bigger than her bedroom at home. And it looked not dissimilar to her own.

She was sitting on a single bed in one corner and there was a chest of drawers for clothes, a desk and a chair and a closet in the opposite corner. On the floor was a bean bag chair.

It was a like a bad dream. Like someone was playing a cruel trick on her and suddenly her sister was going to jump out and scare her. Except she was already scared.

No one came for a long time. Could it have been a whole day? She wasn't sure because there was no window and no clock. It felt really long and she had fallen asleep again.

There must be stairs nearby because she heard the sound of descending footsteps and froze in place on the bed. What should she do? Try to run?

The sound of locks being opened, the clicks and slide of a bolt, echoed in the room and the door slowly moved on its hinges into the dark space behind the room. She could only see a figure and it was carrying a large bag.

'Hi,' said a woman.

She said nothing.

The woman walked towards the desk and switched on the little black lamp sitting on its surface. She could see now that it was same woman from the playing field, the one who had helped her into the car and stroked her hair.

'I know you must be frightened,' she said. 'But you don't need to be. It will seem strange at first, but you will love it here.'

The woman smiled encouragingly at her.

'You must be hungry. I've brought you a feast!'

The bag was actually a large insulated picnic hamper and her stomach involuntarily groaned as plastic containers of food were brought out, their lids opened and arranged on a plate on the desk. It smelled delicious.

'We don't usually have fizzy drinks in this house — they're not good for you. But I thought as a special treat...'

She pulled out a can and pulled back the tab. The crack of the metal opening seemed to ricochet through the room — it sounded like a gunshot and the hiss of the liquid seemed to go on forever.

She told herself to not be scared, to save herself, to run. What was she waiting for?

She was up and off the bed, sprinting through the door that the woman had walked through and all she was faced with was a small, bare hallway that had three doors. The one she had just come through, one right in front of her and another to the right of the room she was being held in. She frantically tried both handles and they were locked.

She shouted out. Her voice echoed back towards her.

There was nowhere to go.

The woman did not follow her. The girl could hear her humming to herself in little room.

She moved slightly to her right so she could see back into the room where the woman was. She had finished setting up the meal on the desk and was now sitting in the chair facing her. She was smiling.

'You're just perfect,' the woman said. 'Louise has always wanted a sister.'

# TWENTY-EIGHT

The list of missing girls wasn't all that Bobby Sharma had discovered. When the results finally came back from Nick Tuft's laptop, there was an internet search buried in the data from three weeks before Grace's murder that confirmed their worst fears.

There had been a search for a kidnapped and missing twelve year old. But it wasn't Grace Feist. Grace clearly knew how she had been taken. Why search for yourself except for your own curiosity? And why risk someone seeing that search when you are working so hard to hide your true identity?

The internet search was for Caitlin Black.

———

Luke, Hana and Nicolson had sent the team home — there was a fine line between exhilaration when cracks were found in a case and pure exhaustion from the exertion of getting there. They had reached that point and the three detectives needed to debrief. Luke had suggested heading to his house.

When they arrived, Hana having ordered a curry from her

mobile phone while they were in the car on their way there, it was clear that Nicolson had never been to Luke's house in Arlington Square.

The house that looked like all of the others on the square with the front door that appeared exactly the same as the ones on either side of it opened into a vast entranceway that immediately revealed that one house was, in fact, two houses knocked through.

Nicolson didn't say anything but she made a slight whistling noise and she shrugged off her coat.

'You should see it in daylight,' Hana said, pointing above them to the giant glass roof.

'My wife had great taste, what can I say?' Luke said, picking up the post that had been dropped through the letterbox and placing it on the table next to his front door keys. Luke and Hana shared a quick glance.

Hana and Nicolson settled in at the kitchen table while Luke pulled out crockery and cutlery and beautifully ironed cloth napkins and lay them out.

'I'm going to open a red, any takers?'

'White, please, Luke,' said Nicolson, pulling a folder out of the tote bag at her feet.

Hana could only smile and shrug at Luke.

The white was opened and the conversation began, only interrupted by the food arriving. They had come to the conclusion that both Grace Feist and Caitlin Black were taken by the same person. It was too much of a coincidence otherwise and the girls had clearly been held somewhere together.

'Which means...' Hana began.

'Yes,' said Nicolson.

'If Grace Feist was released by her abductor, was Caitlin Black released as well?'

'And is she still alive?'

---

The folders that Nicolson had brought along to Luke's were not the ones she had at home in Sussex. They were details that Rowdy had hastily pulled together at the end of the day, as much as she could find about the disappearance of Caitlin Black.

'Did you both work on this case as well?' Hana asked.

'No,' said Luke. 'But I think you did Philippa?'

'I did,' Nicolson said. 'But it didn't garner the same attention as Grace's disappearance. It was one of those cases that got lost and forgotten about quite quickly, I'm sorry to say.'

'Why was that?'

'To put it as bluntly as possible, Caitlin didn't come from a family like Grace's. She grew up on an estate further north, up towards the motorway and she had also been in and out of foster care. She actually wasn't reported missing for almost a week. No one seemed to know — or to care — where she was.'

'Jesus,' said Luke.

'I know. And I'm going to guess with what we know now that this case was not one of our shining moments. The Met isn't going to look good here if we are correct in our assumption.'

'What were the circumstances surrounding her disappearance?' Hana asked.

Rowdy's files were pretty basic. Caitlin Black was twelve years old and at the time living with an aunt in a one bedroom flat in a tower block. Nicolson remembered visiting the block and the sad, desolate feeling of being surrounded by concrete and poverty. There weren't many good ways out of this kind of life.

There had been no bedroom for Caitlin — she slept on a pull out sofa and there was no sign she even lived in the flat apart from a few personal possessions. There were no posters on the wall, or clothes hanging in the cupboard. Only a duffel bag and a large rubbish bag filled with some jumpers and shoes and gym kit. Caitlin often played truant at school and when Nicolson and the other detective with her interviewed her teacher, Nicolson remembered how dismayed the teacher was. She had said that Caitlin was clearly extremely bright and hard working when she bothered to turn up. The teacher had tried to involve a previous foster parent, and then Caitlin's aunt, in her studies. She had tried to encourage Caitlin and spent extra time with her outside of lessons, but the teacher felt what many do at a certain point. That as bright as a pupil is, sometimes the situation is simply futile.

'How does a girl just fall through the cracks like this?' Hana asked.

'I know. We should have done more,' said Nicolson. 'But it begs an important question.'

'What's that?' Luke asked.

'If Caitlin Black was kidnapped, and then released, and is still alive, would she want to be found? Grace certainly did not, for whatever reason.'

'Sisters,' said Hana.

Luke and Nicolson were not following. Luke asked her what she meant.

'Sisters have a bond. I don't know how to explain it. We found a picture of Emily hidden amongst Grace's things in a secret compartment she had made. Rachel told us how much Grace talked about her older sister, Caitlin. Well, what if the reverse is true as well? What if Caitlin felt about Grace the same way?'

'And she just saw Grace's murder on the news,' said Luke. 'Maybe now she wants to be found.'

# Twenty-Nine

The small plastic card landed on Luke's desk with a gentle thwack.

'There you go,' said Henry MacAskill. 'Mission complete.'

Luke picked up the card and stared at it. It was an orange plastic bank card, the name Owen Smith stamped across the bottom of it, under its magnetic chip. Luke ran his thumb over it.

'Well done, Henry. Now...sit down and tell me how you did it.'

Henry looked pleased with himself.

'I'd actually never done this myself but asked a colleague. I'm working with a young chap who is very clever and probably going to take my job at some point soon. He looks about sixteen, although he's in his mid-twenties. I hate him, really.'

Luke laughed and looked at the card again. Henry explained how it was done. And it turned out to be pretty simple.

'It's the same process if you're a little under eighteen or over eighteen. Doesn't matter. You need a piece of official, government accepted identification. And if you don't have a driver's license or a passport, you can get a Citizen Card. Lots of kids have them for when they turn eighteen and want to be able to buy alcohol or get into a club.'

'Do you need to apply for a Citizen Card in person?' Luke was hopeful.

'Nope. You need a photo — easy. You need to pay online with a bank card, or through the post with a money order — easy. And if you don't have any other government issued ID, then you need to have a referee sign the form to confirm that the photo matches who you are. Also, really easy.'

'Explain how the referee thing works?' said Luke.

'Sure. A referee has to be someone in a certain profession that can be contacted at their place of work. A doctor, nurse, lawyer, dentist, social worker — someone like that. And it was fairly straightforward for my colleague to find someone, shall we say, indiscriminate, to confirm his false identity.'

Luke was shocked at how easy this sounded. It would probably be out of the capability of a frightened eighteen year old Grace Feist, but it was completely achievable to do this on her behalf — by her abductor.

'There's one more thing,' said Henry.

'The Citizen Card needs to be posted somewhere — to the address used on the form. And I had the feeling that when you asked me to figure out how to do this, you wanted a scenario that left no traces. Nothing that could be tracked down easily.'

Luke felt a rush of gratitude for Henry MacAskill. He wished that he could tell him what they were dealing with, but he would be able to eventually.

'That assumption would be correct,' said Luke.

'My colleague used a different address to his own. He happens to be living next to an empty flat at the moment and used that address. The post comes into a communal mailbox, and he just took the card when it arrived. At that point he applied for the bank account with the Citizen Card and the fake address, but he could easily have gone online and changed the addressed to his real one at that point without any further ID checks.'

Luke was flabbergasted. It was too easy.

'How did I do?' asked Henry with a grin.

'Perfect marks. This is enormously helpful. Thank you.'

'Anytime.'

The two men sat in a slightly awkward silence — Luke wanting to tell him what exactly this information meant and Henry desperate to hear it.

'Off the record, Henry.'

Henry nodded.

'All I can tell you now is that we believe Grace Feist was living under a false identity and had been freed by her abductor at some point over the past few months.'

Henry's mouth dropped open. Even for a seasoned journalist, this was bombshell news.

'Oh my god, Luke. Are you serious?'

Henry had a thousand questions he wanted to ask. He could feel the story forming in his head, the order of the words he would want on the page when he wrote it. But he knew not to ask Luke Wiley anything further, stood up to shake Luke's hand and left.

———

Philippa Nicolson had been keeping the Feist family up to date with the developments of the case, as delicately as she could. She had not yet told them that Grace had been standing across the street from their house just a few days before she was killed. Nicolson did not think that Rosamund and Jamie Feist could bear this news. To have their daughter almost home again, and then snatched away so cruelly was a burden that they would likely have to bear eventually, but not yet.

There are things a detective never forgets about difficult cases and the Feists, in the horror of Grace's abduction six years ago, were grateful for the hot chocolate that officers would bring them. It was such an anomalous detail — the unspeakable devastation of a missing child and the warm, sweet treat in a cardboard cup.

On this cold morning where the coziness of autumn had passed into the dreariness of winter, Philippa had arrived at the Feists' house with three steaming cups of hot chocolate picked up from the cafe on the high street a couple of block from their home. Buried with Philippa Nicolson was the knowledge that Grace had been so close to her mother only days ago. She felt a twinge of guilt as she handed over the hot chocolate and she tried to push the feeling away.

Nicolson sat in their living room with Rosamund. Emily had chosen to go to school that day after being absent and staying in with her family when the news about her sister broke. But friends beckoned and the routine of a normal sixteen year old's life was a comfort. Her parents, however, felt differently.

'Who the hell took that photo of Emily and how did Grace have it?' Rosamund asked.

The concern was etched all over her face. Was someone following Emily? Was another one of her daughters in danger?

'I don't want her out of my sight, Philippa. It took me years to feel comfortable with Emily going out with friends and not being with us at every moment after Grace was taken. It feels like all of that has been erased now.'

'We think it's extremely unlikely that Emily is in danger. The working theory is that the photograph was a threat and sent to Grace as a reminder to not come home to you or there would be consequences.'

'And the consequences would be the death of my other daughter?' Rosamund's voice was raised and shrill.

'It's just a theory,' said Nicolson.

Rosamund welled up and as she had done for the last few days, allowed the tears to flow freely and without hesitation.

'Do you think that Grace actually saved Emily somehow? By not coming home?'

'I don't know,' Nicolson said, but wondering if this really was the case and how brave Grace would have been to adhere to this instruction. How much she loved her sister.

When Grace Feist went missing, the media attention had been overwhelming to the family. It had not taken long for their home address to be known thanks to unscrupulous journalists, social media and neighbourhood gossip that spread their location far further than this little pocket of north London.

Flowers were placed outside their front door, candles were lit on the pavement outside and for weeks people would stand outside in the beautiful summer weather, often late into the evening, as a kind of vigil for the missing girl. The majority of the attention was sympathetic — that feeling of helplessness, of relief that it wasn't happening to them — and there was a sense of protectiveness and anger that this could happen to a lovely family in north London who didn't deserve such anguish. But there were also the inevitable sick jokes and cruel taunts that found their way to the home of the Feist family.

There were letters that said the sender was holding Grace. Some asked for money, some described what they were going to do to her. There were notes slipped through the door that contained a multitude of vicious and dreadful things.

All of them were collected by the police and examined. There was the slimmest of possibilities that one of them could be real and every avenue was explored. A couple of people were charged with harassment and fined. But eventually as the case grew cold, the notes petered off and the Feists now only received about a dozen a year. They had stopped telling the police about them and simply put them in a bankers box that sat in the closet in their guest bedroom. It was easier to not think about it.

Philippa was still trying to go back to basics in how she approached this case and after her conversation with Hana and Luke she was convinced that it was Caitlin who was the key to unlocking the mystery of six years ago as well as Grace's murder. They had to go back in time. How far back, Nicolson wasn't yet sure.

'Rosamund, I'd like to take a look at your box of unsolicited notes and letters. You haven't been in touch with anything out of the ordinary about them lately.'

'What are you looking for?'

'I'm not sure yet,' Nicolson lied.

# Thirty

Down the hall that morning in the Incident Room, on her fifty third attempt, Joy Lombardi finally struck gold. At a Travel Inn out by Heathrow Airport, a helpful receptionist had gone through their records from two months earlier and found an Emma Jones who had checked into the hotel and paid for seven nights with cash.

Even luckier, this particular Travel Inn kept their CCTV footage for three months, one month longer than customary for the hotel chain, owing to its proximity to the airport and a Border Security request.

'Thank god for the Home Office and their love of bureaucracy,' said Luke as Rowdy was setting up the video feed of the footage in the Incident Room.

'What was Grace Feist doing with so much cash?' Hana asked, to no one in particular.

When the footage came up they fast forwarded through what looked like an exceptionally boring day at the reception desk. The stream of guests was steady and it was clearly busy at this hotel, but the staff didn't look like they were having a ton of fun.

'Imagine dealing with an entire shift worth of jet lagged, cranky travellers and complaints about not having fast enough wifi or slow room service,' Luke said.

'Uh Luke,' said Hana, after he had commiserated with the staff standing behind the reception desk they were staring at on the screen, 'I don't think this is the kind of hotel that has room service.'

There was a ripple of quiet laughter in the room. Luke was still focused on the images in front of him as they watched the time stamp spin forward, still no sign of Grace Feist.

It wasn't until close to eight o'clock in the evening that the team finally saw what they had been looking for. It was an incredible relief to see Grace Feist walk into view. She had been a ghost they were chasing, one that Philippa Nicolson had been chasing for six years. But there was so much sadness in the room as well. There she was — six years older than the twelve year old girl who had been taken. What must she be thinking when she walked up to the reception desk? What had happened to her during all of these years?

And Grace Feist was not alone.

They had not expected this.

Luke paused the footage and walked closer to the screen.

There was a man standing next to Grace. Was he with her? Or was it simply busy at the hotel and his presence was a coincidence, something not consequential to their case at all. He was of average height, in a baseball cap which was pulled down, his face obscured slightly. It was difficult to get a good look at him. His jacket collar was bright cream and looked like sheep's wool.

Luke pressed play on the footage again and that is when they all saw it. The man placed his hand on Grace's back, and then moved his hand around her right shoulder, pulling her towards him in a little hug. A movement of affection.

The man pulled his wallet out and cash was counted and

then accepted by the receptionist. A key card was handed to Grace, who had a backpack at her feet, and then the man turned to leave. He faced Grace and there was a moment or two before Grace turned in the opposite direction with her key and her backpack and left the screen frame.

'He said something to her,' said Nicolson.

'Or vice versa,' Luke replied.

'We need to speak to that receptionist.'

———

Once it was determined that the receptionist in the footage was the same one Lombardi had spoken to earlier in the day, Officer Parker was sent to collect her. Luke looked at the board in front of them and felt both pleased and irritated that it was now rapidly filling with information. Thank god that they were being able to fill in the cavernous gaps that appeared the moment they pulled the body of Grace Feist out of the canal — there had been so many questions, as if they were building a puzzle piece by piece but didn't know what the image looked like yet.

But Luke was irritated that with all of this information, they didn't seem to be any closer to catching Grace's killer. They didn't even know if this was the same person who had kidnapped her six years earlier.

'Who wants pizza?' said Hana, from across the room.

'I could eat,' Sharma replied. 'And I eat anything.'

'Perfect.'

Luke hadn't answered, seemingly oblivious to the debate about what type of pizza was about to be ordered and whether chicken on a pizza should be allowed at all.

'Why keep your bank card in your boot?' he suddenly asked out loud.

'Oh you are here with us,' said Hana. 'What kind of pizza do you want?'

'What? I don't care.'

Hana looked over at Rowdy and raised her eyebrows.

'Wiley,' Rowdy snapped. 'You know what you're doing right? If you don't specify your pizza preference, we're going to be stuck with Hana's choice.'

Sharma looked up in alarm.

'What's that, Ma'am?'

'Only the perfect pizza, Sharma. Pepperoni, jalapeño peppers and pineapple.'

The look of horror on Sharma's face made Rowdy laugh out loud.

'We're not having that,' said Luke. 'One vegetarian. One Meat Lovers. Thank you, Rowdy.'

Luke tapped his pen on the table in front of him.

'Hana. The bank card. Why would Grace have it in her boot?'

Hana sighed and tried to ignore her growling stomach.

'You're a man, Luke. You don't think about your bag.'

'What?'

'Help me out here, Lombardi?'

Lombardi smiled and was happy to chip in and explain what she assumed Hana's theory was to Luke.

'Well, Sir, when you go out for an evening, where do you have your wallet?'

'In my trouser pocket, or in the inside pocket of my jacket if I'm wearing one.'

'Exactly,' said Hana, jumping in and then sitting back in her chair with a gesture of apology for Lombardi to continue.

'Women don't really have that option. Either we don't have pockets, or our wallet is too bulky, or we are also carrying a bunch of other stuff — our phone, lipgloss, hand lotion, a brush, mints, a compact. Whatever. And all of that needs to go in a bag. But if I'm going out at night and I think it's going to be a bit late when I'm coming home, then I try to leave the house with just my phone and bank card. And maybe my lip gloss...depending on the evening,' Lombardi smiled.

'So you think she was worried about being mugged?' asked Luke.

'Yes,' said Hana. 'And I think whoever killed her took her phone.'

Luke turned to ask Nicolson if this theory chimed with her and then realized that she wasn't there.

―――――

Nicolson had asked Rowdy to find her a quiet room to work in for an hour or so. Sometimes this was hard to come by on the seventh floor, so Rowdy had booked her into a small meeting room one floor above them.

The banker's box of notes and letters posted to the Feist Family over the past few years lay open on the table in front of her. She had wanted privacy to go through them. It was difficult to read letters that were, in many cases, ugly and depraved in their content. It was harder still, strangely, to read the notes of support and words meant to comfort the Feists. Nicolson had taken this case very personally six years ago and now that she definitely knew that she had failed to bring Grace home to her family, she was devastated.

And she was angry.

Each piece of correspondence had a hastily scribbled date on the envelope - sometimes on the front, most often on the back — always in Rosamund Feist's handwriting.

Nicolson knew what she was looking for — she just didn't know when it would have arrived. She started opening the letters from the most recent and working her way backwards in time.

She opened a folded piece of paper that did not seem to have an envelope with it. There were two handwritten sentences on the page.

*Grace is fine and will come back. Please wait for her.*

Nicolson turned the paper over. It was dated two years earlier. If she was right, Caitlin Black was released by her kidnapper and living under another name for the past two years.

# THIRTY-ONE

It was terrifying for Grace to never know what time it was, or what day it was. In the first few days, she tried to guess but then began to panic. She was in a constant state of panic. Where was she? Who was this woman? What were they going to do to her?

She needed to be ready to escape, she told herself. She didn't know which of the two doors she encountered in the hallway outside of the room where she was being kept led to the outside, but she decided to try the one next to her if she got the chance.

Every time she heard the footsteps coming towards the door, she froze. She wondered if this time she would be killed.

But the woman was always bringing something to her. A hot meal, some books, a teddy bear. Grace didn't understand, but she was learning that to be obedient was keeping her alive.

She desperately missed her parents. She wanted to talk to her sister. She needed her own bed and her own pyjamas. She lay on the bed in the dimly lit room and tried to imagine walking through her house. What the door handles felt like, which way the door swung open. The sensation of the carpet under her feet in the sitting room, what the curtains looked like.

She was trying to hold onto her life and she was praying that her family would find her soon. She knew they would be looking.

Yesterday the woman had told her to call her "Mama" and this terrified Grace. She couldn't do it. She couldn't bring herself to play along with whatever this scary game was. She wanted her own mum.

The sound of the key being inserted into the padlock and the scraping noise of the bolt that held Grace prisoner were very loud. The woman opened the door and light flooded into the room. Grace shielded her eyes and backed away into the corner of the room.

'Today your Mama has a special treat,' the woman said.

Grace swallowed.

From behind the woman stepped a girl.

She looked a little older than Grace, with long blonde hair and was very pale and thin. The girl stared at her in surprise and then suddenly smiled.

'This is Louise.'

The girl blinked and slowly stepped around the woman and into Grace's room. She slowly looked around, taking it all in.

Grace wanted to scream for help but something made her stay quiet. She told herself to think quickly, to be smart. If she could befriend this girl who must be the daughter of the woman, she could get help that way.

The woman smiled at the two girls and then left the room. The door shut and the bolt slid back across. The key was turned and the lock clicked.

The pale, blonde girl did not turn around in horror at

being locked in the room. She didn't react at all, but just stared at Grace.

Finally, she spoke.

'Hi,' she said. 'Don't worry. They're probably going to call you Louise, too. My real name is Caitlin.'

# THIRTY-TWO

When Officer Parker brought the hotel receptionist into Scotland Yard, she was wide-eyed and smiling. She couldn't believe that her incredibly boring day had morphed into something this thrilling.

Hana and Luke took her into the interview room on the seventh floor, and got her a cup of tea.

'Thanks so much for having me in,' she said, breathlessly.

Hana leaned forward in her chair, not sure she had heard correctly. This may have been the first time someone had been dragged into the Serious Crime Unit and thanked the detectives for the invitation.

'What's your name?' Hana asked.

'Amanda,' the receptionist said.

'Thank you for coming in, Amanda,' said Luke. 'We thought it would be a bit easier to talk here than on the phone. And we wanted to go through the CCTV footage with you. We hope it can jog your memory a bit.'

'It's Grace Feist, isn't it,' Amanda said quickly, the words bursting out of her mouth. 'That's who you think was at my hotel.'

'Yes,' said Luke. 'We think she stayed there a couple of months ago. You said she stayed for a week.'

'I don't really remember how long she was there, but she paid for a week.'

'And why do you remember her specifically?' asked Hana, suddenly aware that this receptionist might be too eager to insert herself into the search for Grace's killer.

'Because she paid in cash,' Amanda said. 'That's really unusual.'

Luke pulled up the CCTV footage on the laptop screen and swivelled it around so the three of them could all see it.

'Let's have a look at this. Can you fill in the blanks for us? Did Grace walk in with this man? What did each of them say? Things like that,' he said.

The images were a little grainier than the detectives would have liked but they watched the interaction back and Amanda was nodding as she watched.

'So,' she said. 'I don't remember if they had a reservation or not. Sorry. But I know that her dad said this was a treat because she was starting a new school program or something nearby and he was paying for a week until she moved into her accommodation.'

'How do you know it was her dad?'

'Um, I don't know. He may have called her his daughter. Or I just assumed. Sorry, I can't remember.'

'Did Grace say anything?' Hana asked.

'I think she just said thank you and bye. Nothing that would be out of the ordinary.'

'It was a good couple of minutes that they were standing at the reception desk talking to you. You don't remember anything else that was said?'

'Oh sure. I had a conversation with the dad about the cash.

I still needed a card on file with the room booking to cover any kind of incidentals. Like damage or if a guest uses a premium video service on their tv. But he didn't have a card on him.'

'So what happened? Grace still checked in,' Luke said.

'The dad promised to come back with a card. I really shouldn't have let him do this, but I figured that his daughter was staying for the whole week and he wouldn't *not* come back and see her or deal with it. And he did come back.'

'He did?' Luke and Hana said, simultaneously.

'Yeah. A couple of days later. He gave me a card to put on file and he also left something for her.'

'One second,' Luke said, standing up and striding towards the door of the interview room. Hana knew exactly what he was doing and could feel the flutter of excitement rising in her chest.

Luke ran down the hall towards the Incident Room and burst through the door.

'Sharma. The kidnapper had to file a card at the Travel Inn and did it two or three days after the date Grace checked in. Get the...'

Luke didn't even need to finish his sentence. Sharma was already up and on the phone and using his free hand to furiously key instructions into his laptop. If they had the name of the card holder, they'd get him.

Down the hall in the interview room, Hana suddenly realized that Amanda had said two things.

'What happened when he came back with his card?'

'He let me tap his card so we had it in our system with a payment hold and he left an envelope for his daughter.'

'Did he say anything about the envelope?'

'No, only to make sure that she got it.'

Hana felt unsettled and tried not to show it. She thanked Amanda for coming in and escorted her back to Parker who would finish getting all of her information.

Entering the Incident Room, she walked over to the board and picked up the marker. Luke, who was still hovering over Sharma's laptop, looked up at her. She pulled the cap off the pen and wrote under the Travel Inn column that had been created.

**Kidnapper dropped off photo of Emily**

'You're kidding,' Luke said.

'Grace had this photo hidden in her room, printed out on a piece of paper. I believe it was a threat. He was saying: I can see your family, so don't you dare go back to them or I will know.'

'Can someone cross reference the date that the card was used at the hotel and this photo was dropped off with the date the doorbell camera was installed opposite the Feist house?' he asked.

'On it, Sir,' said Lombardi.

Luke stood in front of the board with his arms crossed. Why did he feel like they were gathering good information and everything was clicking into place, but they seemed further from Grace's kidnapper — and killer — than they were days ago.

Nicolson had slipped quietly into the room and was taking in the new information that everyone was staring at. There was one remaining slice of vegetarian pizza left and she picked it up and took a bite. She hadn't eaten cold pizza since she had retired. She thought that maybe she missed it.

'You can add something else,' she said, startling the room.

'Philippa, sorry, didn't see you come in,' said Luke.

Nicolson took another bite of her slice and tossed the half eaten piece of pizza back in its greasy box. She wiped her hands on a piece of kitchen roll that someone had thought to place next to the food. Then she opened the file folder next to her and pulled out the photocopy of what she had found in her search one floor above everyone.

Under the column on the board that held Caitlin's name — the emptiest space on the board — she affixed the note.

'Shall I do the honours?' she asked, to no one in particular. 'This was posted by hand through the Feists's letterbox almost exactly two years ago. It is a handwritten note and says: *Grace is fine and will come back. Please wait for her.*'

The room was completely silent. It was Hana who finally broke it.

'Surely not. You don't actually think...' She trailed off, unsure exactly of what she was going to say, what she should be figuring out with everything on the board in front of them all.

'Oh I do think so, Sawatsky. I think Caitlin Black was abducted eight years ago. I think the same kidnapper took Grace Feist six years ago. I believe the girls were held together and formed a tight bond. And two years ago Caitlin was released. For whatever reason she did not go to the police or contact anyone that she knew. But she did try to let Grace's parents know that Grace was alive and would also be released. And then Grace was.'

'That's got to be a hell of a reason,' said Luke.

'Yes,' replied Nicolson. 'And something went wrong. I believe that Grace did something she shouldn't have. And it got her killed.'

# Thirty-Three

The feeling that Grace had was one she had felt once before, the first time she went to away to camp. It had been only a long weekend — four days — but she didn't know anyone and was instantly homesick. As much as she tried to focus on the activities that she was supposed to be participating in during the day, all she really wanted to do was go home. She felt out of place and slightly queasy and wanted the trip to be over.

On the second day, she made a friend who was sleeping in the same cabin as her. They became inseparable for the rest of the long weekend because there was solidarity in a pair. Things became less frightening and they felt less strange. With a friend in tow, Grace was able to enter a different kind of reality than the one she was used to at home and the days ended up passing quickly until her parents came and picked her up and it was over.

Finding Caitlin was exactly the same.

Grace's fear never really went away, but as she heard Caitlin's story she felt both relieved that it didn't appear that she was going to be hurt, but she felt sick to her stomach that

Caitlin was there, too. Because Caitlin told her that she had
been in the locked room next to her own for the past two
years.

On that first day when she was brought into Grace's room,
Caitlin would not stop talking. She asked dozens and dozens
of questions. Some of them were about what had just
happened.

Where was Grace when she was taken? How long did she
think she'd been here? Where was she from and what school
year was she in?

And then Caitlin peppered Grace with desperate questions about the outside world. Who had won the football
league this year? Did any famous actors get married or die?
Did she watch a specific television program and what were the
characters up to? Did this band release a new album? Did it
snow last Christmas?

Did the world know that Caitlin was missing? Was
everyone looking for her?

At these questions, Grace somehow knew that she should
lie. She had never heard of a missing girl called Caitlin, but
how could she tell her that? And she knew that everyone
would be looking for her, which meant that Caitlin would be
found at the same time, so the lie didn't feel like a very big lie.

In the midst of Caitlin's interrogation, she began to detail
what it was like living in the locked room.

'My room is right next door and looks almost exactly the
same. Eventually you will get a laptop. There's no wifi or
anything but there are games and some school lessons that are
pre-loaded and lots and lots of DVDs to watch. Some are old
and a bit boring, but I don't know what to ask for that is new,
obviously.'

The calmness with which Caitlin was describing what
would happen to Grace was terrifying. Would she also be here
for two years?

'I really hope that we will be able to stay together,' Caitlin said.

Grace began to cry and whispered, 'Me too.'

Caitlin moved onto the bed that Grace was sitting on and put her arms around her.

'It's okay. No one is going to hurt you. I have figured out how to live here until we get out of here. Eventually we will.'

'How do you know that?'

'The man promised me.'

Grace swallowed hard. She had hoped that the man wasn't here. She hadn't seen him since she had been put in the car.

'Who are these people? What do they want from us?'

Caitlin lowered her voice and Grace suddenly wondered if they could be overheard.

'They want us to be their children,' she said. 'Just try not to be frightened when they show you the photos.'

# THIRTY-FOUR

If Philippa Nicolson was correct, they had two more pieces of the puzzle. Both girls were released, and two years apart. That would have made both girls eighteen years old when they were set free. What happens at age eighteen? Why then?

The second piece made her feel heartbroken, but she wasn't yet sure where this piece fit. Grace had come to her old home. She could have walked across the street and rung the doorbell. She could have tried the handle and just walked through the door. She could have shouted for her parents that she was home.

In the doorbell camera footage, she hadn't lingered long. She would have seen the gnome that she had picked out with her father six years earlier, just the weekend before she was taken. What would she have thought? Did she understand that the garden ornament was kept there as a beacon for their daughter? That it was saying: we are here, we have not forgotten you.

'This is maybe what Grace did wrong,' said Luke.

He and Nicolson had taken a break from the Incident

Room and walked down to the pub. It was still a couple of hours before last orders but the place had already begun to empty out. This was a drinking hole that catered to people who worked in this part of Westminster. Lots of government employees, the accountants and insurance brokers that populated the building next to the Met, and lots of tired detectives who needed a pick me up between leaving the office and heading home.

Nicolson was nursing a white wine and Luke had ordered a coke. He wasn't in the mood for a beer and didn't dare chance a vodka gimlet in this kind of pub. He would probably be laughed out the door.

'You think that Grace was threatened with her life if she went back to her family?'

'I think that's the most likely explanation at this point,' said Luke. 'What I don't get, though, is how you motivate a frightened teenager who you kidnapped and held for six years to stick to that bargain.'

'I'm going to guess that she went through something terrifying. Fear is an extraordinary motivator.'

'Do the Feists know that Grace was on their street this week?' Luke asked.

'They do not.'

'They are going to have to know at some point, Philippa.'

'I know,' she said, taking another sip from her wine glass. 'But I can't quite bear it at the moment.'

Luke understood this completely. He wouldn't want to tell them either.

'Is Richard okay with you being back in London for the foreseeable?'

Nicolson smiled and ran her fingers up and down the stem of her wine glass.

'I think he's probably enjoying the peace and quiet. Richard got quite used to my absence from the house when I was working and it's still an adjustment for him now that I'm retired.'

'And how has the adjustment been for you?' asked Luke.

'I don't know what I was expecting. What did you expect would happen when you left the Met?'

'My circumstances were a little different, Philippa.'

She reached over and squeezed his arm. Nicolson wondered what it was like for Luke to have had such tragedy in his own life. For all of the terrible things she had seen in her job — the series of unfair events that happen to people when they are least expecting it and do not deserve them — she had not yet suffered a life altering loss. In this moment she wondered if she had been too proprietorial about Grace Feist over the past few days. Perhaps she should be letting Luke steer their direction more, let his own experience guide them further into the quagmire of clues that weren't yet leading them where they needed to go.

'This really does feel like old times,' said Luke. 'It's been nice having you back.'

'I do like Sawatsky,' Nicolson said, leaning back in her chair.

'Do you? I'm glad.'

'I think I may have made her a bit nervous.'

'Hana? I highly doubt that. I've yet to see her nervous about anything. Quite the opposite actually. When we began working together, I was a bit worried that I'd have to reign her in a bit.'

'I had Rowdy pull her file for me,' said Nicolson. 'And I told her.'

'I'm sorry, you did what?' Now Luke was laughing. He could just picture it. Nicolson interrogating Hana about her past. Good luck with that, he thought.

'You don't think I've put her off a bit, jumping back into

the fray with the two of you. Three can be a crowd when it comes to detective partners. I remember the feeling.'

'I don't think so, Philippa. If there was anyone more secure in herself and her job than DS Hana Sawatsky, I've never met them. Hana will be fine.'

'That's good. And I also poked Rowdy for a bit of insight into how *you* are doing, Luke.'

'Oh yeah? And what was Rowdy's report?'

'She said you are a fucking mess.'

And with that quip, Nicolson downed the rest of her glass just as Luke's phone began to ring.

———

Nicolson's dramatic little speech with her theory in the Incident Room had, in fact, rankled Hana immensely. She also knew that she was being unfair. It wasn't Philippa she was irritated at, it was Luke.

Since they had collected her from her house in Sussex, Nicolson had been nothing but professional and, Hana had to admit, interesting. She understood where Nicolson was coming from — if Hana had a case that went unsolved, and it had involved a missing girl and a grieving family — she would have jumped right back into where she had left off, too.

And that was the thing. Philippa Nicolson had never left the case behind. Hana was a couple of decades away from retirement and for the first time ever, she had wondered if this is what her future may look like.

She liked Nicolson. Was it a bit cheeky to have Rowdy pull a file on Hana and then let Hana know she'd done it? Absolutely. But Hana had enjoyed their drink and she understood that Nicolson had done it to make her feel like she was on Hana's side.

But at the moment, she didn't feel like Luke was on her

side. She felt that their usual balance had been altered and he was paying far more attention to what Nicolson was saying about this case than what Hana was bringing to the table.

It was an unfamiliar feeling and it pissed her off.

Hana had left the Incident Room and was back at her desk. She was beginning to find the room claustrophobic and she couldn't think properly in there. Hana had picked up where Luke had left off with the bank card that Henry MacAskill had brought in that morning, another situation that made Hana feel slighted.

Ordinarily, Luke would have discussed this approach with Hana before asking Henry for this favour. She knew that the two men were friends, but he had, quite purposefully, inserted Henry MacAskill into this case and probably given him more information than a journalist should have at this point in the investigation.

And how helpful could figuring out how to open a bank account under a false name really be to them? Luke had relayed to the entire team what Henry had explained the process had been to get the bank card. If this was, in fact, the same way Grace — or someone helping Grace — had become Emma Jones with the ID and the bank account to match, then the referee would probably be fake, too. The address for the Citizen Card could be absolutely anywhere.

Nevertheless, she had spent hours on the phone earlier in the day, speaking to official after official on the administration team of the governmental body that stores the personal details of Citizen Card applications. It had been tedious, but Hana had been happy to spend time out of the Incident Room and had finally worked her way up the hierarchy to speak to someone who could actually help her. The personal information was stored, she was told, and Hana would be emailed both the name and place of work of the referee and the original address used on the application. They would probably arrive in her inbox separately. Hana had thanked the woman and then put it out of her head. The rest of the day had been taken over by Luke and Nicolson and the shock of what was possibly Caitlin's message to the Feist family.

As surprising as a crack of thunder, someone down the hall on the Serious Crime Unit had put their desk phone on speaker.

Her irritation rose even further that someone had accidentally pressed the speaker button so the entire seventh floor had to be subjected to their phone call. But the voice shouting into void of their quiet office was getting louder. The person who had received the call was pressing 'up' on the volume button. Hana stood up to see who it was and then she heard what the voice was saying.

A girl had been snatched from outside a convenience store thirty minutes earlier.

Struggling to understand what this meant, Hana looked down the hall to see Rowdy rushing towards her.

'I've just called Luke. Hana, you have to go. He'll meet you there.'

# THIRTY-FIVE

Whether or not the Metropolitan Police Force was a little jumpier than usual because of Grace Feist, it seemed like every single patrol car in north London had descended upon the convenience store.

Hana had to abandon hers on the adjacent road and make her way to the scene on foot. It was a cold night for standing around and she wished that she had thrown on a scarf. Police tape was up everywhere and she had to flash her badge again and again to get to the store.

As she approached, Hana could see Nicolson leaning over a police car, its backseat door open. She was talking to someone.

Luke was standing on the pavement speaking to a worried looking couple. She waited to catch his eye, but he was deep in conversation and the man he was speaking to was wringing his hands and looking towards the police car.

'Philippa,' Hana said, interrupting the detective.

Nicolson looked up and nodded at her, indicating that she was almost finished. After a minute, she went to join Luke, had a quick word and then walked over to Hana.

Hana told herself to focus. She found herself bristling at the fact that Luke and Nicolson were already here. She knew they had been having a drink in the pub and instead of driving one block over to collect her, they had jumped in their car and driven straight to the scene.

'We have witnesses this time,' Nicolson said. 'The girls are thirteen years old.'

'Girls?'

'Yes, the friend who I was speaking to in the patrol car is a witness. Luke is with her parents. They are absolutely frantic, but nothing compared to the parents of the girl who has been taken. I've had support officers take them back to their house and we'll head there now.'

'Poppy Travis. We have given out her description and details of the car that took her. It's flooding social media and we've made the ten o'clock news. We'll find her.'

'What exactly happened?' Hana asked.

'Both girls had been at Poppy's house which is only five minutes from here. Unbeknownst to Poppy's parents, they decided to hop on their bikes and ride over here to buy some crisps. The friend said they thought they wouldn't be missed. She was hysterical. They cycled over around 8:30pm.'

'Was Poppy taken from inside?'

'No,' said Nicolson. They didn't have locks for their bikes, so the friend went inside to buy what they wanted and Poppy waited outside with both bikes. When the friend came outside, she said that the bikes were lying on the ground and Poppy was gone.'

'CCTV footage?' Hana asked.

'Nothing from the store. Poppy must have been lured over to the car somehow. But we got lucky. A food delivery guy on a scooter saw the entire thing. He was the one who called the police. He was on the phone before the friend was even out of the store.'

'Shit, I wish he'd just followed the car. Did he get a plate number?'

'No. But it's good information.'

'Hana,' Nicolson said in a low voice, stepping towards her. 'It's our guy.'

'Ma'am, with all due respect, the timing of this could be a coincidence and nothing to do with Grace.'

'No,' came the reply. 'The witness described what the guy was wearing. He had on a jacket with a sheep's wool collar. Same as the hotel CCTV footage. It's our guy.'

Hana's mouth dropped open.

'Oh my god.'

'I know,' said Nicolson. 'But this time we're going to get him.'

————

The atmosphere at Poppy's house was unlike anything Hana had experienced before. She had never before worked an active child abduction.

Luke knew this and came towards her as soon as she walked through the front door.

'Come with me,' he said.

She followed Luke into the kitchen, which was quiet and so tense, it felt as though the glassware sitting on the countertop might shatter of its own accord from the pressure in the room.

Every time a mobile phone rang, Poppy's mother jumped out of her chair and waited for it to be answered by her husband. Was it Poppy? Was there news? Did they have her?

It was excruciating to watch.

'Look, there's not much we can do here. I'm going to see if Nicolson can stay with the parents and you and I can head back to the station.'

Reading between the lines, Hana knew Luke was saying that Nicolson was the person best equipped to handle panicking parents. She had been here before.

'I feel helpless,' said Hana.

Luke didn't want to let on that he felt exactly the same way. He felt himself beginning to panic, which was unlike him. The kidnapper had been brazen and that was not a good sign. When Caitlin and Grace were taken, it felt calculated and clever. No one had seen and he had chosen his location and timing well. There had been a plan that had been executed and twice in a row he had pulled it off.

But this time the snatch felt desperate, as if Grace's death hitting national news had spooked him. Who knows what he would do with Poppy at this point?

'Best thing we can do is keep going with what we have. There is someone out there who can help us,' said Luke. 'I have the feeling that if we find Caitlin Black, we're going to find Poppy Travis.'

'It's a needle in a haystack, Luke,' said Hana.

'No,' he shook his head. 'It's right in front of us.'

As they walked back to where they had both parked their cars, Luke could see the television crews, their camera lights flashing in the dark and the boom mics hovering above some of them. It was quickly becoming a scrum.

'Do you think that's going to help us or hurt us?' Hana asked.

Luke thought of Henry MacAskill and how he might be able to plant a seed for Caitlin Black to find. Hell, he'd even use Toby Peacock if he thought it would work. Hana was clearly thinking the same thing.

'Why not make an appeal for information about Caitlin Black? We need to find her.'

'There's just no way, Hana. Can you imagine O'Donnell if we even suggested this? We let the public know that not only did we not find Grace Feist and she was released and then murdered, but there was another woman who was abducted and released before her?'

'I get it,' said Hana. 'And there's something else, too.'

'What's that?'

'It would be deeply irresponsible to reveal that Caitlin Black was alive, having gone through the trauma of the past eight years, without her permission. She would become headline news herself, and she clearly hasn't asked for that if she has been able to live anonymously under another name for the last two years. It would also potentially be extremely dangerous to her.'

'If Philippa is right,' added Luke.

Hana nodded.

'I wish that I thought she wasn't. But I think she is.'

Hana's mobile phone began to vibrate in her pocket. After the events of the last few days, she braced for Luke's mobile to ring as well, but it remained silent. She pulled out the phone and saw that it was Sharma.

'Sawatsky,' she said.

They had reached Hana's car and Luke leaned against the passenger side door, waiting to hear what Hana was going to say. She was listening intently until she thanked whoever was on the other end and hung up.

'It was Sharma,' she said, opening her email on her mobile and scrolling through the messages until she found what she was looking for.

'Did the name or address of the bank card used at the hotel come through?'

'No, sorry. Not yet,' Hana said, still reading the email on her screen.

'So what is it?'

Hana clicked the side button on her phone to darken the screen and slipped it back into her pocket.

'The referee for Emma Jones' identification has come in. I didn't think that it would be real but Sharma has checked it out and this person does actually exist. It's a woman. A nurse who used to work at the Royal Free Hospital.'

'Used to work?' asked Luke.

'Apparently, the brilliant government official who is supposed to check the referee doesn't actually speak to them. They just check the hospital records. And this woman did work there for several years. I'm sure it's just the name that is being used and this person would have no idea what they've been embroiled in, but I should check it out anyway, don't you think?'

Luke shrugged, which made Hana bristle once again.

'Why don't you head back to Scotland Yard,' she said. 'The Royal Free is on my way back there. I'll stop in briefly in case anyone remembers her.'

Hana didn't wait to hear Luke's response. She opened the car door and within a few seconds had turned on the ignition, pulled around her partner and driven away.

# THIRTY-SIX

Hospitals were not one of Hana's favourite places to visit. When she was a child, her mother had undergone a host of surgeries and treatments for a particularly grim cancer and her memories of visiting her mother in one were thoughts that she tried to push away.

She still felt the slight rise of panic in her chest when she walked into a hospital, and that was before the usual sterile, clinical atmosphere took over. There was nothing joyful about a hospital. The antiseptic smell only heightened your awareness that this was not a natural or welcoming place to be. It was instead a place of sickness and pain and misfortune.

Hana hadn't rung ahead. She decided to ask around when she got there and to try to track down someone who may have known this nurse from years earlier. She entered the hospital through the emergency ward and was directed through it into the centre of the building.

Trying not to look at the patients on gurneys, shielded only by thin blue curtains, she made her way to the main administration desk which, even at this time of the evening, was busy with two staff members fielding calls and sitting in front of mounds of paperwork.

'What was the name again?'

'The nurse was called Marjorie Tennant,' Hana said.

'Do you have any idea which department she worked in? There are a lot of nurses at this hospital.'

'The only other information I have says "Surgical Ward".'

'Okay, well I'm not sure we can help you. But you're welcome to try the main nurses station on that floor. It's on five.'

Hana thanked the staff and headed towards the lift, wondering if Luke had been right and this was a futile exercise. She should be in the Incident Room trying to track down Caitlin Black, not searching in vain for an old employee whose name was probably lifted by the kidnapper and stolen for their own perverted use. But if there was a chance that the nurse had a connection in some way to whoever took Grace Feist, then this detour back to the station was worth it.

In contrast to the bustling din of the emergency department, the surgical ward at this time of the evening was quiet. The nurses shift change had already happened, their first patient rounds had been completed and the nurses were checking charts and sipping from cups of water and tea at their central nursing station in the middle of the unit.

Hana introduced herself and asked if anyone had known or worked with Marjorie Tennant. Mostly blank faces stared back at her question but one nurse suggested that her colleague might know. Nurse Drake was on a break and getting a bite to eat in their break room one floor below.

Thanking them, Hana was relieved to be heading off the ward and slipped into the stairwell to head down and find Nurse Drake. After being directed to the break room, she knocked softly and let herself in.

The only person in the room was a woman in her sixties

with short hair and wearing bright pink scrubs. She looked exhausted.

'Nurse Drake?'

'Yes?'

Hana introduced herself and apologized for intruding on the tired woman's break.

'That's okay,' Nurse Drake said. 'If I'm not here working, I'm home looking after my grandchildren and not getting any rest there either. What can I do for you?'

'I'm trying to track down a nurse who used to work here. Her name was Marjorie Tennant. Do you remember her? The nurses upstairs said that you've been here the longest, so you may have worked with her.'

The nurse whistled through her teeth. Hana wasn't sure what this reaction meant, but smiled at the woman, looking perhaps a bit too hopeful.

'That's a name I haven't heard in a long time,' she said.

'So you did work with her?'

'Sure. I worked with Marjorie for a couple of years. She was an excellent nurse. When she was here.'

'What do you mean?' Hana asked.

'She was absent a lot. And always last minute. At the time it really pissed me off. You thought you had a day off and then all of the sudden your supervisor is ringing you to say that you have to come in and cover a shift. And it was always Marjorie's shift that we were covering.'

'How long ago was this? When did you work with her?'

Nurse Drake thought about Hana's question and did some calculations on her fingers.

'It would have been about ten years ago now. Doesn't feel that long.'

'Ten years and you still remember being angry about Marjorie taking sick days. That's interesting.'

Nurse Drake took a sip of hot tea from the mug in front of her and swirled the liquid around in a circular motion.

'It wasn't Majorie who was sick. So really, I'm being unkind. You should forgive me. I'm tired tonight and I just remember how tired I was back then, too.'

'Sorry,' said Hana. 'Can you explain?'

The nurse nodded and took another sip of tea.

'It was her daughter. She had a little girl who was always really unwell. And out of nowhere. Marjorie was extremely protective of her, always worried, always wanting to be home with her. I used to tell her that she should bring her daughter in here, get a second opinion about whatever was going on. The Royal Free is one of the best hospitals in the country. But I don't think she ever did. In fact...'

Nurse Drake stopped herself short and Hana leaned forward in her chair.

'What?' she said. 'What were you going to say?'

'Oh it's silly. I shouldn't say it, shouldn't repeat it. But I remember one of the other nurses who worked with us at the time was also angry about Marjorie not showing up for work all the time. She thought the whole thing was made up and that Marjorie was deliberately hurting her daughter so that she could spend time with her.'

'Hurting her how?'

'Look, I shouldn't be saying any of this. Marjorie probably works at another hospital now and I don't want to give her any trouble.'

Hana considered her options here, and she didn't have many. She needed this information and she needed it now.

'I'm sorry that I can't give you the detail about why I'm asking you to tell me everything you know about Marjorie Tennant. But it's almost midnight and I'm here speaking to you when this usually would be done at more sociable hours. Please tell me.'

The nurse took a moment and then shrugged her shoulders.

'Look, a few times I — and some of the other nurses — caught Marjorie taking things from the medication cupboards. Syringes, vials of various description. No one said anything and I have no idea if any of this is connected or important, but it happened. And then her daughter died.'

Hana couldn't believe what she was hearing.

'When?'

'She left the hospital soon after it happened, so I guess around ten years ago? She was distraught about it. Obviously. I know her husband was as well.'

'Do you know who her husband was?'

'No idea, sorry. I never met him.'

'Do you remember his name?'

The nurse shook her head.

'One day Marjorie was here and then the next she wasn't. She just left. We all assume that she went home.'

Hana looked confused.

'What do you mean?' she asked.

'I assume she returned to France. Marjorie was French.'

Hana wasn't sure she thanked the nurse properly. She was running down the hospital corridor, jamming her thumb onto her phone screen as she skidded around the corner and into the stairwell. There was no time to wait for the lift. But the time she was at her car, Luke had picked up the call.

'Luke,' Hana said breathlessly. 'I'm on my way back. We've got something.'

# THIRTY-SEVEN

Although the woman let Grace and Caitlin spend most of their days together, when she came downstairs, she liked to see them one at a time. Grace was always relieved when it wasn't her turn.

The woman would enter the room quietly and if Grace was already awake and up, she would be instructed to get back under the covers and sleep. Grace learnt quickly that she had to pretend and close her eyes until the woman would begin to sing softly in French.

Then she would sit on the edge of Grace's bed and begin to rub her back, her shoulders, and then long strokes down her arms and her legs. Grace hated being touched by her, every hair on her body standing up in revulsion. But it got worse.

Although there was a small basin in the corner of Grace's room, on the days that the woman came, she took Grace into the hallway and through the door that led to the rest of the house. Another antechamber was there before a further locked door and this housed a bathroom with a toilet, sink and bathtub. The bath was usually run before Grace was led there and the woman began to remove Grace's pyjamas.

She had tried to do it herself once, tucking her fingers into the elastic of the pyjama bottoms and sliding them down her legs. The woman had slapped her across the face with a ferocity that made Grace shout out in shock and pain. The side of her face became raised in a red welt that lasted for over a day.

Grace was lowered into the bath and she had to hope that the temperature was reasonable. If it was too hot or too cold, the woman did not listen to her protestations. It was as if the woman went into a kind of trance during this ritual and did not hear her at all.

She was scrubbed with a rough cloth. Every inch of her. Then she was wrapped in a large, fluffy bath towel and brought back into her room. The woman would sit Grace on the bed, still swaddled in the towel while she went over to the chest of drawers and began to pull out clothes. Just before she was taken, Grace had started wearing a bra, but one was never offered to her. Only underwear, socks, and an outfit of trousers and blouses. There were many bright, colourful jumpers. Sometimes Grace was pulled into leggings that felt too tight and a grey pleated skirt with a waistband that cut into her middle. Although a range of shoes were in the cupboard, Grace never put them on.

Once dressed, Grace was instructed to sit on the floor in front of the bed while the woman sat behind her. Grace's hair was brushed and braided.

'We have to grow it long, long, long,' the woman murmured to her, every single day.

Bobby pins were clipped in and adjusted and then the worst part of the morning began.

'Are you ready for Louise?'

Grace never said anything. There was nothing to say.

The woman patted the bed next to her. Grace knew not to protest.

The photos were always the same. They all featured the same girl. She was dressed in clothes that now lived in Grace's chest of drawers in this locked room. The girl had long blonde hair, done up in a double French braid at the back. She was lying in a bed in a pretty bedroom with flowered wallpaper and lovely cream bedding that looked soft and inviting.

The girl was dead.

She was lifeless, even in the still photograph. Her skin was so pale it had a blue tinge to it and her lips were the wrong colour. Her eyes were wide open, staring at nothing.

# THIRTY-EIGHT

The activity in the Incident Room had become frantic. No one had gotten any sleep. In a period of three hours the previous evening, they had been given their first sighting of the kidnapper, a description of his car, and what felt like the first concrete piece of the puzzle — a name, and possibly a motive.

Sharma had been busy running the name Marjorie Tennant through every database he could think of. He found the daughter almost immediately. Louise Tennant had died almost exactly ten years ago. The cause of death was heart failure. She had been twelve years old.

'Heart failure in a twelve year old?' said Hana.

Rowdy did some more digging and came up with associated medical files and now they had Dr. Chung with them, looking over everything. Dr. Chung rarely came up to the seventh floor, usually being visited in her lab one building over. She had certainly never been in the Incident Room and was gawping at the board, now covered in handwriting, images, and a bunch of theories.

'What do you think?' Luke asked her. 'Anything in that file of use?'

'This girl was constantly ill. And there doesn't appear to be any consensus about what was wrong with her. She kept being tested, for basically everything. There is a note here that perhaps the girl should undergo psychiatric testing.'

'I don't think this poor girl needed to see a shrink. But her mother certainly did,' said Hana. 'Is there anything else?'

'The only other diagnosis is high blood pressure. Again, that is very unusual for a twelve year old. Her bloodwork showed a high level of carvedilol.'

'What is that?' Luke asked.

'It's a beta blocker. A medication that functions to slow down the heart rate. It's a very common drug, but not for someone this age typically.'

'And what would happen if a twelve year old was administered a lot of this drug?'

'Her heart would stop.'

The moment Dr. Chung uttered these words, the entire room looked up at her, and then at Luke.

'Are you saying what I think you're saying, Wiley?' Chung asked.

Dr. Chung looked over at the television monitor that had been set up in the room the previous evening. It was tuned to BBC 24 hour news and the only news at the moment was the abduction of Poppy Travis. They were racing against time and the race was feeling increasingly tight.

'I'll leave you,' Dr. Chung said. 'You know where I am if you need me.'

Nicolson had appeared just as Dr. Chung was speaking to the room and she hovered in the doorway.

'Good morning, Philippa,' Dr. Chung said to her old colleague, as she made her exit.

'You caught that?' Luke asked.

Nicolson nodded and scanned the room.

'Coffee, Ma'am?' said Lombardi.

'You read my mind. Please.'

'Did you get any sleep?' Hana asked her.

'Not really. I left the Travis family around 2am, but I wasn't exactly tired. I should have come in here but it seemed like you had everything moving where it needed to move.'

'We're getting there,' said Luke.

Lombardi had poured Nicolson a steaming cup of filter coffee from the machine in the corner. It was terrible coffee, but it would do. Nicolson waved off the offer of milk and sugar. She would have taken the coffee intravenously at this point if she could.

Luke moved a half empty cup of coffee slightly further down the table and then hopped up to sit on it.

'Okay,' he said. 'Shall we go over our working theory? We need to work quickly here. I don't feel good about Poppy Travis. We can't lose her for years like the other two girls, and who knows what this couple is going to do now with this much media attention.'

'Hold on,' said Hana. 'You're definitely sure that we are looking for a couple? And even if we are, there was enormous media attention about Grace Feist's disappearance and they released her.'

'And then I think they murdered her,' piped up Nicolson. 'And I'm agreeing with Luke here. We are looking for a couple. I really think we are. I think that — thanks to Hana — we know that Marjorie Tennant was obsessed with her daughter, very possibly made her ill, and then accidentally or not, killed her. So she went looking for a replacement daughter.'

'That her husband abducted for her? Three times now?' said Hana. 'It fits, but it's still a stretch, no?'

Sharma yawned and scratched his head.

'Here's the thing I don't get with this theory,' he said. 'Why release the girls?'

'Because they're kind hearted kidnappers?' Hana blurted out. 'I don't know, Luke?'

Nicolson was sitting very still, looking pensive. The room seemed to turn to her, hoping for another answer, another way forward that made more sense to them all.

'Maybe they aged out,' she said.

'Sorry?' asked Hana.

'Louise Tennant was twelve years old when she died. Both Caitlin and Grace were twelve, or thereabouts, when they were taken. Maybe these two girls got too old eventually, so they were let go.'

'And given a brand new fabricated identity by their attackers?' Hana began to laugh.

The atmosphere in the Incident Room felt too tense, too hard to navigate. Theories were one thing, hard evidence was another. And they needed more of it. Luke didn't jump to Nicolson's defence, but neither did he side with Hana's doubt. He didn't know what to think.

'Sharma,' he said. 'There must be a husband linked to Marjorie Tennant — can you find him?'

'Not yet, Sir. There is no marriage certificate, nor is he listed on any of the paperwork for Louise's death. It's possible that they didn't marry in England, if Marjorie is French. I think our best bet is to wait for the details on the card he used at the Travel Inn to come back. I'm expecting them this morning.'

'Can you get them, Sharma. We are running out of time.'

Nicolson had stood up, still holding her mug of coffee and walked up to the board. She peered at the copy of the second piece of paper they had found in the plastic sandwich bag, taped to the bottom of Grace Feist's bedside table drawer.

'Back to basics,' she murmured to herself, although the entire room heard her.

Nicolson tapped the piece of paper.

'This list of churches. Where are we with it? Anyone? There has to be a reason it was hidden.'

A room full of blank faces looked back at her.

'We are assuming that Grace was looking for something. Probably Caitlin, right?' said Hana.'

What are we supposed to do, search every church in London? If she is even in London? There aren't that many churches on this list, so Grace hadn't got to very many.'

Nicolson nodded in a sort of truce with Hana. She was right. This seemed impossible.

'Sir,' Sharma said suddenly, still staring at his laptop screen. 'I have it. The card used at the Travel Inn. And an address.'

Luke grabbed his coat and headed towards the door.

'Let's go,' he said, to no one in particular.

Nicolson and Hana looked at each other until finally Hana gestured towards Luke, who was already halfway down the hall, Sharma texting him the address that he hadn't even waited to hear. Nicolson finished her coffee and then followed Luke towards the lift.

# Thirty-Nine

No one dared to use the showers in the basement of Scotland Yard. They weren't particularly nice and usually only visited by those fitness fanatic officers who jogged to the office.

Hana was not one of those people.

But it had been a long night and she had a change of clothes in her desk, kept there for emergency all-nighters like the once she'd just had and she was desperate to feel hot water wash away as much of what she was feeling as possible. So to the basement she went.

The shower actually wasn't that bad and it was a scalding temperature, just how she liked it. She couldn't relax under the spray of water like she could at home, even on the hardest days. There was just too much to do and a ticking clock and Poppy Travis needed to come home. There was enormous responsibility suddenly lifted onto her shoulders with a case like this, and it was making Hana feel exhausted.

She had to admit that Nicolson was right — they were missing something that was probably right in front of them. What couldn't they see?

Instead of heading straight back to the Incident Room, Hana decided to get some fresh air. She ran a brush quickly through her hair and tossed the brush back into the bottom drawer of her desk.

'Want to join me for breakfast, Rowdy? I'm going to head to the cafe and get something to go.'

'No, I'm okay, Hana. But thanks. Why don't you stay in cafe and sit down to eat? Take a few minutes.'

What would the department do without Rowdy, Hana thought. Getting the detectives anything they needed, often understanding what this was before even they did, and also acting as mother to the unit.

Hana decided to take her advice while she waited to hear what Luke and Nicolson had found at the address linked to the bank card. The cafe was busy at this time of the morning and Hana thought she would have to grab something to go anyway, and then she saw an arm waving in her direction.

It was Henry MacAskill.

Hana didn't know Henry as well as Luke did, but she liked him. She walked over to his table.

'Morning, Sawatasky. Join me?'

Hana looked around and the seat across the table from Henry was one of the only empty spots.

'I'm not going to talk about Poppy Travis. Too sensitive,' Hana said.

Henry raised his arms in the air in mock surrender.

'Hey, I'm just having poached eggs. Off the clock.'

'Okay,' Hana laughed. 'Thanks.'

It was nothing out of the ordinary to see a detective and a journalist eating breakfast together in this cafe next to Scotland Yard. And the conversation between the two was pleasant and not particularly invasive. Lots of chat about the current state of the Met, the sports scores, the weather.

When Henry asked Hana how Luke was getting on now

that he was back at work, she thought that this line of questioning was just like the conversation that had preceded it. He was asking a routine question out of politeness, perhaps with a dash of curiosity thrown in.

But the next question made Hana put down her cutlery, and almost choke on her toast.

'What exactly do you know about Luke's wife's death?'

It was an odd turn of phrase. Why refer to Sadie's death, instead of Sadie's accident? It was not the usual word that people used when discussing what had happened.

'What do you mean, Henry?'

Henry shrugged in a way that only heightened Hana's unease.

'I mean what were the exact circumstances? How did she go off the road like that?'

'Why on earth are you asking me this?'

'I'm sorry, Sawatsky. This isn't the time. You're just trying to grab a bite to eat and get back to finding Poppy Travis. And figuring out what happened to Grace Feist. I don't mean to distract you.'

Before Hana could open her mouth to reply, Henry had taken three twenty pound notes out of his wallet and tucked them under the sugar canister on the table.

'Breakfast's on me,' he said, and then he was up and out the door.

—————

Hana did her best to shrug off the conversation and she made sure to get the change from the note. Pocketing the five pounds that was handed back to her by the server, she was stopped by a tall, looming figure the moment she walked out the door.

'DS Sawatsky, hello.'

Hana looked up, squinting slightly in the light, even though it was a dreary, overcast morning.

'Oh, Officer Parker, it's you.'

Parker smiled sheepishly at her.

'Sorry to bother you, but I saw you through the window having breakfast. Didn't want to disturb until you were done.'

'Oh,' Hana said again. 'You were waiting for me or...?'

'It's just that it's my day off today and, obviously, I saw the Poppy Travis news last night and I just wanted to know if you needed any help.'

Ordinarily, this kind of unsolicited approach and interruption in the middle of Hana's day would have thrown her into a quiet rage. But this was not an average day and she thought *why the hell not.*

'Come on up, Parker. I'll sign you in. The more the goddamn merrier.'

Parker needed no introductions when they entered the Incident Room. Everyone was happy to see him.

Sharma leaned back in his chair, clearly not having slept at all yet. Stifling a yawn, he handed a piece of paper to Hana.

'What's this?'

'It came in about an hour ago — the address that was used in the application for Emma Jones' Citizen Card.'

'Has there been any word from Luke or Nicolson?' she asked.

'Yes, no luck on their end. The couple at the house were almost expecting the police to turn up at their door. Not for Poppy Travis, but because it keeps happening. Identity theft. It was a dead end. They're on their way back now.'

Well in that case, Hana thought, why not give herself a bit more space and check out this address.

'Where is it, Sharma?' she asked, looking down at the piece of paper.

# FORTY

Hana plugged the address into the GPS and checked the directions. The route would take her east of here, out towards Barking and it would be about a thirty minute drive. The route also would take her right by her house.

She had moved to east London five years earlier, just before she began working as Luke's partner. Although she called it a house, and it technically was, it was down a small mews and only had one bedroom and one bathroom. It was more flat-sized than house-sized and she liked to joke that she could fit the entire place inside one of Luke's walk-in closets.

It was probably only a slight exaggeration.

But it was hers and she loved it and it had taken every penny she had to buy it, and now stressed her out with a size-able mortgage. Buying her own place also meant that for the first time since she lived at home as a teenager and was no longer in university digs, or in military accommodation, or renting from testy landlords, that she could get a cat.

Having spent the previous night at the scene of Poppy's abduction and then Scotland Yard, she hadn't gone home to feed Max. She debated pulling in and turning right when she passed her road, but decided that she would do it on the way back to the station.

Her mobile rang and she glanced over to see that it was Luke calling. She let it ring through to voice mail and then tucked the phone into her cup holder.

The density of the brick houses through Shoreditch began to ease the further east she drove, into the more industrial areas around Canning Town and then to the rows of detached houses on the outskirts of Barking.

The American voice on her GPS, that always made her giggle in the way he mispronounced many British road names, announced that her destination was on her right, so she pulled over and parked. She leaned forward and looked through the windshield towards the houses. If pressed to describe them, her immediate thought would have been that they were nondescript. This wasn't going to take long, but at least she'd been able to clear her head a bit on the drive.

She opened the car door and stepped out. There was the smell of a wood stove in the air. In front of her the houses all looked identical and she checked the address again that Sharma had handed her. Finding the correct house, she looked at the front window — there was only one — and tried to determine if anyone was home. There were a few cars parked on the street, but looking down in between the houses, it looked like most of them had detached garages in their back gardens. It was the kind of neighbourhood that had more concrete than grass and the entire area felt a bit downtrodden.

Hana walked up to the front door and pressed the doorbell. She didn't hear any corresponding chime from inside the house, so she pressed it again. Hana waited.

She knocked loudly on the door and leaned over to look inside the front window, but it was covered with an opaque curtain.

Another dead end, she thought, and she went to return to her car.

The front door to the neighbouring house opened and a woman walked out in her dressing gown, two empty wine bottles in her hands, which she placed with a clank into the recycling bin that sat out in the open in front of her house.

'Good morning,' Hana called to her.

The woman hesitated, staring at Hana, and the curiosity got the better of her.

'What do you want?' she said.

*Charming*, Hana thought, as she walked across the concrete slab that sat in front of both of these homes, its cracks sprouting weeds that would soon be as tall she she was.

Hana took out her badge and held it up, as she identified herself.

'Do you know your neighbour?' Hana asked.

'Yeah,' she said. 'Why? What did he do?'

'What's your neighbour's name?'

'I have no idea. He's not exactly friendly. Geoff? John? Jack? No idea.'

'How long has he lived there?'

'I was here before him, that's for sure,' the woman said. 'His wife isn't very nice either.'

'Has there been some kind of conflict?' Hana asked.

'Just a hell of a lot of noise when they moved in. Construction. They got planning permission to build out their basement. All of us were against it. None of us have a basement and once one house gets permission, everyone else is going to want to do it. I spoke to the council about it.'

'When did they build the basement?'

'I don't know. When they moved in. My friend down the road here — a couple of houses down — she said that they built a swimming pool down there. Can you imagine? A pool at your house? Here in Barking? Ridiculous. Awful people.'

Hana suddenly wondered if the neighbour was drunk at eleven o'clock in the morning. She was rambling on and Hana was struggling to make sense of what she was saying.

'Sorry, can you repeat that? A swimming pool? Are you sure?'

'I've never seen it,' the neighbour said. 'He never talks to any of us. But my friend saw the concrete that was being poured in and her husband works in construction and she said that it looked like it was for a pool.'

The neighbour was still muttering to herself as she went back inside, leaving Hana standing in front of the houses, staring back at herself in the reflection in the glass window.

The brightness of the day had suddenly turned and heavy drops of rain began to splatter on the concrete at her feet. Hana looked back at the car. Then she turned and walked towards the rusty metal gate at the side of the house. It was quite a high gate and she had to stand on her toes to reach up and over it to release the latch on the other side. The gate creaked as it swung open and Hana walked along the side of the house. Looking up there were no windows on this side either, although the house on the other side of her had them.

It must be really dark inside, she thought as she ventured into the back yard. There was nothing in the backyard at all, just more concrete and a single car garage at the end. The neighbour must be mistaken. There couldn't be a basement here.

There were two windows on the back side of the house that matched those of its neighbours, and the same opaque curtains hung in them. It didn't look like anyone lived here.

Hana walked around to the garage and tried the door. To her surprise, it was unlocked and she lifted it up and peeked inside. The garage was empty but there was a strong smell of petrol, as if a car had only recently been driven out of it. The door was heavy but Hana was able to lift it completely open, and light flooded into the small space.

There were some shelves that held a toolbox and a petrol can and some tubes of expanding foam. Usual garage detritus.

Had a car been parked in the garage, Hana wouldn't have seen it. There was a door in the floor directly underneath where the car would be. It looked like a cellar door with a large metal handle sticking out of it.

Hana bent over and had a good look. She had never seen anything like this in a garage. She pulled the handle upwards and the door began to open.

The door was incredibly heavy but she was able to yank it open where it stayed open at a 45 degree angle on a retractable hinge.

What the hell was this?

Crouched on her hands and knees, Hana peered inside and could see half a dozen steps leading into some sort of hallway. She reached into her pocket for her phone and felt nothing. She silently cursed her phone still sitting in the cup holder of her car and eased her foot onto the first step.

It seemed sturdy so she swung her other leg over and eased herself into the hole. Descending one stair at a time, very carefully, the air around her immediately felt different. It was cold and slightly musty and it smelt almost metallic.

She reached forward in the pitch black space and her hand grasped nothing but air. The door suddenly made a loud clicking noise as the hinge gave way, slamming shut above her.

# FORTY-ONE

Luke and Nicolson were disappointed with their dead end. They arrived back at Scotland Yard feeling like they had just wasted a huge amount of time. Poppy had been missing for just over fifteen hours and every single person in the Incident Room felt the clock ticking like it was connected to a bomb, ready to go off at any moment.

'Sorry,' Rowdy commiserated as they poured themselves a cup of coffee.

Luke nodded and looked around at the room.

'Where's Hana?'

Sharma looked up from his laptop.

'The address that was used to get Grace's fake Citizen Pass came in and she went to check it out.'

'Okay,' said Luke. 'Anyone hear from her yet?'

'Not yet, Sir,' said a voice from the corner of the room.

It was Officer Parker and Luke was surprised to see him.

'Parker, what are you doing here?'

'It's my day off, Sir. I thought I could make myself useful.'

Luke couldn't help but smile at the young officer. He

admired his ambition but also wondered how much of his presence was due to wanting to see a certain Hana Sawatsky.

Poor guy, Luke thought. He has no idea what he's setting himself up for.

Nicolson sipped her coffee and it did nothing to ease the feeling of dread that had settled in her stomach. Unless they got a call from a member of the public who had seen the car the kidnapper used, or seen Poppy Travis and had more information, they didn't have much else to go on. It was a terrible feeling, and one that she didn't think she would be forced to feel again after the Grace Feist case.

She stared at the list of churches on the board in frustration. If the list was so dangerous and needed to be hidden, why couldn't they see what it was for?

'Anyone figure this out yet?' Nicolson said, pointing to it.

The room was completely silent except for the rustling of papers and gentle clacking of fingertips on a keyboard. The television displaying the news on a loop on the other side of the room was set to mute.

Officer Parker looked around at the room and cleared his throat.

'Parker?' said Luke. 'What is it?'

'Is it the list of churches that you are asking about, Ma'am?' he said.

Nicolson eased herself off of the side of the table she had been leaning on and stood up.

'Yes,' she said. 'Does it mean something to you?'

'It's a list of Anglian churches,' Parker said. 'With choral societies.'

'Can you explain?' Nicolson said.

Parker looked around the room once more, suddenly aware that everyone was staring at him.

'Sure,' he said. 'I hope I'm not interfering at all. It's just that DS Sawatsky brought me up here and said I could familiarize myself with everything and I spent some time looking at what you had on the board. And the churches just jumped out at me. There aren't that many Anglian churches in London that have choral societies.'

'How do you know this?' Nicolson asked. She had walked back up to the list and was staring at it.

'I sing in one, Ma'am,' Parker said, looking embarrassed.

Nicolson swivelled around to face Officer Parker.

'You brilliant man,' she said.

Parker didn't quite know what to do with that statement, but he smiled at her and said something that had been bothering him since he had looked up all of the Anglian churches with choral societies in London after noticing the list.

'I'm not sure if it's relevant or not, Ma'am,' Parker said. 'But that list. There's one church missing.'

———

Luke called Hana as he and Nicolson were in the car driving to St. Mary's Church in Brixton Hill.

Luke and Hana did not leave voice mails for each other. There was never any need. The person who missed the call would simply see the other's name on their phone screen and dial back. Or would text.

But for some reason, this time Luke left a message. He explained where he and Nicolson were heading and why and asked Hana to meet them there.

'She's still not picking up?' said Nicolson.

'No.'

'Maybe she found something useful at the address.'

'Maybe,' Luke said.

At St. Mary's, the two detectives walked to the front entrance, but it was locked.

'I thought churches were always supposed to be open?' Luke said.

Nicolson headed down the street a little bit and around the back of the building and Luke followed. There were some people milling around, mostly young men and several of them were smoking.

'Excuse me,' Nicolson said. 'Is there someone in charge we can speak to?'

The men looked blankly at them and didn't say anything but just shuffled their feet. One of them silently pointed towards the door.

'Inside,' he said.

Luke and Nicolson opened the back door to the church and stepped through it. There was a small recreation room, decorated with children's drawings and handmade cards featuring psalm verses. There was the smell of stale coffee and musty prayer books.

Luke could see the vicar towards the front of the room next to a door that seemed to lead into the church itself. It was a woman vicar, her hair in a multitude of braids, held back by a purple ribbon that matched the shirt she was wearing under her cassock, its long sleeves just visible at her wrists.

She was speaking to a young woman and an older man who looked like he was part of the group standing outside.

The vicar noticed the detectives and came over to speak to them. She explained that St. Mary's was assisting a group of Congolese refugees, looking nervous that they were there for a reason related to immigration.

They reassured the vicar that they were not, and Nicolson began to ask if the choral society had any members who were young women in their early twenties. But before she could finish asking, Luke had walked over to the young woman, with her back to him. She was speaking to the man in French.

'Caitlin,' he said.

Although no one had called her by that name in almost two years, instinctively, she turned around.

# FORTY-TWO

When she was set free, Grace wanted to see her family. Of course she did. But after spending four years with Caitlin, and then missing her more than it was possible to describe when she suddenly disappeared, she wanted to see her more. It was an unbreakable bond.

For almost two years Grace had wondered if they had killed Caitlin. She wept for weeks after Caitlin had vanished. But when Grace was released and she was not harmed, she knew that Caitlin was out there.

When Grace would sit around the flat with Rachel, she pretended to be a normal twenty one year old girl. But she wasn't. She thought about telling Rachel what had happened to her, how she had been locked in a basement room for six years. But how do you describe something that would be abhorrent to anyone else, but that was simply your reality? A reality you had to get used to in order to survive.

There was no way she could describe how she and Caitlin used to have fun. The games they played with each other, the secrets they confessed. The bond of the secret they knew they would both carry for the rest of their lives if they got out of there.

Grace could never admit that there were things she loved about living with Caitlin in that basement. Things that became a comfort.

Caitlin loved to sing. Her voice was unbelievable. Grace told her that she would have won any singing competition she entered. But what Caitlin really loved to sing were hymns.

When her grandmother was still alive, she would take Caitlin to church and Caitlin, with her angelic voice, joined the choir. As the voices soared towards the roof of the church, their voices ascending toward the heavens, she felt a sense of peace that she did not feel anywhere else. And when her grandmother died and she began to move — from her mother to foster care to her aunt — she never stopped signing at church.

The wall between the girls' rooms in the basement was too thick for Grace to be able to hear Caitlin when they were separated. But when they were together, Caitlin would always sing.

And Grace's favourite place to sing was in the ravine that the girls were taken to a couple of times each year.

The first time it happened, Caitlin had been on her own, before Grace had arrived. She told Grace about it, how she had been injected with something that made her drowsy and carried by the man through a hallway and up some steps into a garage. It was the way she must have been brought into the house months before.

Bundled into the backseat of the car with Mama, they had driven somewhere. It didn't seem like it took very long to get there, but they were in the middle of nowhere. There was an old, decrepit house that backed onto a ravine. Over the ravine was a bridge that had been built, no more than twenty feet across.

Caitlin had run. She had sprinted away from the couple,

trying to focus on her feet, how heavy they felt and she didn't want to trip. She didn't want to be slowed down.

But she realized quickly that there was nowhere to run to. The bridge led to a drop of hundreds of feet, the escarpment impossible to scramble down. She may have been out of the locked room in the basement but she was just as trapped.

When Grace and Caitlin began to be taken there together, Grace would run onto the bridge while Caitlin climbed into the pit of the ravine below. The sound of her singing rang up through the small gully, echoing as a refrain back to them. Grace would sing back, making the song as loud as possible.

A chorus of sisters.

# FORTY-THREE

Hana tried not to panic. She went back up the steps to the cellar door and pushed it. The door wouldn't budge. She tried again, the fear beginning to rise in her throat. She wasn't claustrophobic but this was not good.

How could she leave her phone in the car?

Either the door was heavier than she thought or, more likely, the hinge needed to be released by the upward movement of the handle.

The handle that was on the other side of the door.

Hana gingerly put one foot down onto the step lower than the one she was standing on. She outstretched her arms in the pitch dark to try to maintain her balance. There was darkness and then there was a black nothingness and that is where she found herself. It was disorienting and she couldn't remember how many steps there were.

Not that she knew where they led to.

One by one she descended the steps until her foot touched a surface that felt different. It was carpet.

Why would there be carpet in a cellar?

Lowering her other foot, she shuffled forward a few inches, her arms now outstretched in front of her. They still did not reach anything.

How big was this room? Was it even a room? And how was she going to get out of here?

Something told Hana to keep quiet and not to shout out for help. She doubted very much that she would be heard down here anyway.

Hana shuffled forward a bit more and her right hand hit a wall. She brought her other hand towards it and swept them both along the concrete in front of her.

The sound of metal being inserted into another piece of metal made her freeze. It was coming from her left and fear surged through her body, her blood suddenly rushing into her ears. She held her breath.

It was a key turning inside a lock.

A bolt scraped back and clicked into place.

Then it was silent.

Hana braced herself.

She knew she was at a disadvantage. She had no weapon, and no understanding of the space she was in. Could she hide? Could she buy herself some time?

There was no time.

A door to her left swung open with a crash, the light that instantly flooded the room blinding her. It was a like the light from an atom bomb, radiating out in an instant.

She did the only thing she could do. She ran towards it, her forearms crossed in front of her as protection, barreling towards the space behind the door.

But the man standing in the doorway was wearing a head-lamp and wasn't bothered by this difference in light. He caught Hana with one arm and quickly pinned her down on the floor. She bit him, as hard as she could, and he yelled out in pain but did not let her go.

'You bitch' he snarled, his spit hitting Hana's face.

'Hold her,' said another voice, this time a woman.

Hana yelped as she felt the needle sink into the flesh just below her ribcage. She kicked out with her legs, the only part of her that wasn't pinned down on the floor but she felt herself begin to feel heavy and it was an effort to move them.

She stopped resisting, and the man began to drag her into the house, into a small windowless hall that had two doors next to each other. The man reached up to turn the handle of the door on the left and pulled Hana inside.

'She's an adult, do you need to give her more?' the man said.

Hana turned her head towards the man's voice and that's when she saw the figure tucked up in the fetal position on a bed in the corner. The lamp next to the bed was on and the little girl blinked at her.

Hana tried to open her mouth to tell Poppy she was going to be okay but the second needle went into her leg and then everything went dark.

# FORTY-FOUR

Caitlin stood in front of them, here in the church nave, her arms at her sides, very still. She had learned not to cry many years before, even before she had been abducted, when she was taken from her single mother who did her best but struggled, into foster care. And she learned not to cry when her aunt flicked lit cigarettes in her direction while she was sleeping on the pull out sofa.

She did cry those first few nights, gripped in fear, in the locked room in the basement. But she learned to stop crying in that house, too. It got her nowhere and she needed to learn how to survive. That is what she told herself over and over again for more than eight years. You are a survivor.

But when Philippa Nicolson smiled at her, a gentle smile, and calmly said her name, Caitlin began to cry. The tears were unexpected and shocked her, and she could not stop them.

Both Luke and Nicolson were wary of touching the young woman, now almost twenty two years old, unable to imagine the depth of the trauma she had been through.

'We are here,' Luke whispered to Caitlin. 'You are safe now.'

The female vicar was watching from the end of the nave and Luke told Nicolson and Caitlin that he would be right back. He asked her if there was a quiet place that they could take Caitlin to talk and that they would need a couple of hours of privacy.

The vicar did not ask any questions and offered her own study and led Caitlin and the detectives to it. The room was cozy with two sofas in a little nook to the right of the vicar's desk. Caitlin sat down on one of them, then instinctively took off her shoes and tucked her legs beneath her. She knew this would be a long conversation.

Nicolson excused herself briefly to call back to the station and inform the team that they had found her. Hana had not returned yet, but Rowdy was almost breathless as she took in the news and said she would relay it to the others. She knew that the detectives would need to be delicate over the next hours, desperate to extract the information out of Caitlin that would lead them to Poppy Travis.

Nicolson assured Rowdy that the moment they had any relevant detail, she would call it in. She also asked that Hana be sent to their location as soon as she got back.

'Caitlin,' said Luke. 'This is going to be just the first of quite a few conversations we are all going to have, and after this, we will help you with whatever you may need. But we are in the middle of a serious situation that we think only you can help us with.'

Caitlin nodded.

'Before we begin,' Nicolson said. 'Is there anything you would like to ask us?'

'They killed Grace, didn't they?'

Caitlin was biting her lower lip, the look on her face was both pleading and resigned. She already knew the answer.

'We think so, yes,' said Luke.

'How long ago did she get out of there?'

'We believe two and a half months ago,' said Nicolson. 'And if you've seen the news, we believe that whoever took you and Grace have now abducted Poppy Travis.'

Caitlin took a deep breath but it caught in her throat and she coughed. Nicolson got up and went to find some water, returning with a jug and three glasses.

'We are happy to hear anything you wish to say, Caitlin,' Luke said, 'but I'm going to start with a few questions, okay?'

'That's fine.'

'Do you know the names of the people who took you?'

'I don't. I even tried to look them up on the internet when they let me go. But I never knew them. It was a man and a woman who were maybe married, but I don't know. We were told to call her "Mama".'

Jesus, Luke thought to himself. Philippa was right.

'You never heard them speak to each other? You never heard another name used?'

'No. I'm sorry.'

'That's okay,' Luke said.

'What about where you were held?' Nicolson asked. 'Is there anything you can tell us about that? Were you driven a long way from where you were taken? Do you know if it was a house, if it was in a city or the countryside, anything like that?'

Caitlin told them how she'd been taken, how she thought what happened to her had been her fault. She had been playing truant from school, a couple was hanging out close to the park where Caitlin thought she would be meeting up with some friends, but no one else was there. The man was drinking a beer and offered Caitlin one. He said it was in his car, so she walked over and that's when it happened.

'I don't know how long the car ride was because they drugged me,' Caitlin told the detectives. 'But it wasn't out of London. I don't think we went on a motorway, I would have remembered that.'

There were too many questions to ask. If Luke felt like he was bursting with them, he couldn't imagine how Philippa was feeling. She was being uncharacteristically quiet.

'Philippa,' Luke coaxed. 'Is there something that you would like to know?'

Nicolson seemed to be in the same state of shock that Caitlin was — like the ghost she had been chasing all of these years was suddenly in front of her. Except it was the wrong ghost.

'Were you and Grace held together?' she asked.

'Yes, sort of. We had rooms next to each other and had to sleep separately, but spent most days together in one of the rooms.'

'So you had each other.'

Caitlin's tears formed again and began to slide slowly down her cheek.

'Yes,' she said quietly. 'I thought I would see her again. I thought...'

'She was looking for you,' Nicolson said, and Caitlin's head snapped up, her eyes wide.

'She was?'

'Yes, and she led us to you. We just took a little while to figure it out.'

'I tried to let her parents know,' Caitlin said. 'I left a note.'

'We found it.'

'It was the gnome,' Caitlin said. 'I didn't have the exact address but Grace had told me what street she lived on and she told me about the gnome she had just bought with her dad. I felt so terrible when I was let go. It was the only thing I could think of to do for her.'

Luke was worried. This girl was traumatized and they needed more information out of her than she could maybe give them. So far they did not have any details that added to the picture of who these people were or where they were hiding Poppy Travis. He would have to try a different angle, some other way to see if there was anything new they didn't already know.

'Did the woman who kidnapped you teach you and Grace how to speak French?'

Caitlin nodded.

'Yeah, a bit. And then she got us language tapes and books. There wasn't much else to do, so we taught ourselves. And the woman was so happy with us. It made everything easier.'

'Can you talk a bit about what happened when they released you?' Nicolson asked.

'For me, it was two years ago. I was so happy but it felt awful to leave Grace behind. You have to believe me. There was a part of me that didn't want to go.'

'We understand,' Nicolson said gently.

'I didn't get to say goodbye to her. I didn't know that it was going to happen when it did. I mean, the man told us from the beginning that we wouldn't be hurt. But we didn't see him very often, so we were never really sure.'

The entire story was hard to believe — but the detectives did have a lot of it right. Caitlin was given a brand new identity with a Citizen Pass, and she was given £10,000 in cash.

'I had never seen so much money in my entire life,' she said. 'It was like winning the lottery.'

The man came into her room one night with the card and spent the evening explaining how she could get a bank account, a job, what she should do when she was set free.

'I took notes and everything. I wanted to make sure that I told Grace what he had said, but I never saw her again.'

Caitlin wasn't put up in a hotel. She was driven to a hostel and because she had stayed in hostels many times before when her mother was between jobs and between flats, she felt comfortable. She stayed there for almost a month before she moved in with some people she had met there and got a job as a cleaner.

'Caitlin, why didn't you tell anyone what had happened to you?'

The girl was quiet for a very long time. Nicolson worried that she had pushed her too far, that whatever had happened would never be able to be said aloud.

'They would have killed Grace,' she finally said.

'Why do you think that?' Luke asked.

'Because they killed their own daughter. We saw the photos.'

What Caitlin described next was chilling. Photographs of dead Louise Tennant, dressed in different outfits, sometimes in her bed, sometimes propped up at a kitchen table with a plate of food in front of her. Photos of the dead girl cradled in her mother's lap, always with her eyes wide open.

'You have to understand something,' Caitlin said. 'After all of that, I wanted to disappear.'

# FORTY-FIVE

Rowdy had been calling Luke's mobile and he had been ignoring it. They were trying to extract as much information out of Caitlin as possible, as quickly as they could.

Nicolson was still talking to her, trying to figure out what next steps might be for the frightened young woman, and Luke stepped out of the vicar's study to ring Rowdy back.

'Sorry,' he said. 'Caitlin is still talking and we're trying to get the details.'

'I'm so relieved you found her, Luke. But have you heard from Hana?'

'No,' he said. 'She hasn't been returning my calls. She's not back from checking out the address from the fake ID card yet?'

'No, she's not.'

Rowdy paused for a moment before speaking again.

'Luke, I'm a little worried. None of us can reach her. We've been trying for a couple of hours now. And we've been trying non-stop.'

It wasn't like Laura Rowdy to be worried. She was always

the opposite of worried. Luke checked his watch and asked if Officer Parker was still in the Incident Room.

'He is, yes,' Rowdy said.

'Can you have him pick me up from the church? We'll drive out to the address in Barking and take a look for her.'

———

After almost three hours of talking to Luke and Nicolson, Caitlin was exhausted. Luke thought that the vicar's study had probably never received such an incredible confession before.

Caitlin agreed to accompany Nicolson to Scotland Yard for a brief hour of processing, before being introduced to a team of support officers who would spend the rest of the afternoon with her. There would be many more conversations to have, but they had spoken quite enough for today.

Parker arrived at St. Mary's Church and he and Luke began their drive out to the east end of London. He had brought Luke a can of coke and Luke thanked him.

'Can I ask, Sir, what happened when you found her?' Parker said, weaving through the afternoon traffic.

Luke filled him in on the detail, which wasn't strictly following Met protocol but they would never have found Caitlin today if it wasn't for Officer Parker figuring out the specifics of the list that Grace had hidden.

'It's going to be a really tough road ahead for Caitlin,' Luke said. 'It was startling to hear her talk about some truly terrible things that happened in such a calm way. Like she had rationalized everything that had happened to her and to Grace. It was like the two girls were able to construct a kind of normal life for themselves while they were being held. They were even allowed to go outside a couple of times each year.'

'Really?' said Parker.

'Apparently. They were driven not too far away to another

location and were let outside to play in a ravine. The way Caitlin was describing it, it was like a fun outing instead of a chance to escape.'

'Wow,' said Parker. 'Those poor girls.'

Pulling up to the house, Luke immediately saw the familiar shape of an unmarked Metropolitan Police vehicle.

'There she is,' he said.

Luke got out of the car and checked the address that Sharma had given them. There was the house, directly across the street. Luke pulled out his mobile and pressed the button to call Hana. The sound of a mobile phone rang, echoing the ringing on the phone he held to his ear. Luke looked down into Hana's car and saw her mobile in the cup holder, its screen lit with Luke's name flashing on it.

Luke's blood ran cold.

He slowly let his hand drop, both his and Hana's mobiles still ringing. When Hana's phone clicked over to voicemail, he looked through the window again and her phone displayed over thirty missed calls.

'Parker,' he said. 'Something is wrong.'

Officer Parker was on the phone calling the Incident Room before Luke had made it to the front door. He didn't bother to knock. With two swift kicks, the door splintered open and Luke crashed through to the other side.

Pain shot through his right calf and into his knee and he limped into the front hall of the house.

'Hana!' he shouted.

The house was dark, no lights were on and he swiped his phone screen and put on the torch function. There was one sitting room to his right, with a window facing the street. He pulled the curtain open and light flooded into the tiny room. It was dusty and looked unused.

Luke turned to his left and holding his phone in front of him, ventured further into the house. The kitchen was empty, but two plates, still with the remnants of a meal, were lying in the sink. A fly was buzzing around them, the only sound in the house.

Down the hall was a small bedroom and there was the glow of an illuminated screen on a small table in the corner. Luke approached it and saw that it was a computer monitor connected to a black circuit box and a carefully wound mass of wires. There on the screen was the street the Feists lived on, the doorbell footage from the house opposite broadcasting into the room.

That's how they found Grace, Luke thought. They followed her on one of the days she visited her old house, and then they killed her.

His sense of dread increasing with every step he took through the house, Luke continued through the hall to the back of the kitchen. There were two doors in the hall, facing opposite directions. One opened to the backyard and Luke struggled with the lock. The bolt was stiff and it took him a second to release it. He opened the door to see a small field of concrete that led to a single car garage.

The other door was locked, too. But this one had a padlock and it was firmly closed. Luke looked around him for something strong enough to break the lock. Any kind of metal casing, or loose pipe. And then he saw what was at the bottom of the door. Another lock — with a bolt that was drilled into the concrete floor.

*Jesus Christ.*

'Sir!' shouted Parker from somewhere behind him in the backyard.

Luke rushed out the door to see Parker poking his head out of the garage.

'There's something in here,' he said.

The five strides it took Luke to reach Parker felt like they took a lifetime too long. He burst into the garage, expecting to see Hana. Was she tied up? Was she injured?

But all Luke saw was Parker holding open a reinforced cellar door leading to somewhere darker than Luke had ever seen before.

———

It was a relief to hear the sirens getting louder as they neared the house. When Parker and Luke realized they could not get into the basement, Luke called for tactical backup. They were able to break in through both the house and the cellar in under a minute.

Both of the rooms in the basement were searched but there was no one there. One had been stripped of its furnishings, only a cold, barren space with a basin in the corner remained. The other still had a bed with a pink, floral duvet and a lamp with a pretty matching shade. The desk was set up with paints and a sketch pad, both of them unopened and unused. There was a teddy bear on the chair.

Luke could barely breathe.

He needed to get out of the basement. He needed air.

Officer Parker followed him into the concrete backyard, the lights from a police car, flashing across his face.

'The other location, Sir, that you spoke about in the car. Where is it?'

Luke was still holding his mobile phone in his hand and he quickly pressed a series of buttons and brought it up to his ear.

'Philippa,' Luke said. 'Do you still have Caitlin with you? I need you to put her on speaker.'

# FORTY-SIX

Grace Feist could never have known that by searching for Caitlin and leaving a list of churches hidden under the drawer in her bedroom, she would save two lives. Three, if you count the new life that Caitlin had suddenly been given after she was found.

'Do you know why you were taken to this house in another location,' Luke asked Caitlin, once Nicolson had put her on.

'There was a woman there. An old woman. Grace and I never met her, but she may have been Mama's mother. The first time I was taken there, I heard the woman I had to call Mama speak to the older woman the same way. But the woman, whoever she was, was called Berenice. The man called her that.'

They had a name.

And Berenice Tennant is not a common name. Sharma found her death certificate in no time at all, along with the deeds of probate that were filed the following year. The property was now listed under a company name, but they had an address.

The tactical team said they could be there in an hour — the location wasn't too far away. Luke and Parker hopped in one of the vans and rode with them, sirens blasting for the first forty minutes until they were out of London proper and at the edge of Epping Forest. From there the vans kept their speed, but in silence, not wanting to alert anyone to their presence.

The couple were not expecting them. They were arrested without incident and Poppy Travis sobbed as she was picked up by a Met officer and carried into a waiting ambulance.

Luke had rushed into the house, now just a shell with rotten floorboards and puckered plaster. There were a maze of rooms, mostly empty apart from some chairs, a damp sofa, a single grimy mattress on the floor. That is where Hana was found, still not fully conscious, but otherwise unharmed.

The medics were with her and had run an IV. Her pulse was slow, but she was coming around. She saw Luke and cried out, reaching for him with her hand.

Overcome with emotion, Luke gripped it and bit his lip.

'It's okay,' he said. 'We have you. And we have Poppy. You did great.'

Hana could only nod slightly and a tear slid down the side of her face.

Luke didn't know what to say. His relief was enormous, and he wanted Hana to smile, to realize that her ordeal was over.

'You're not going to believe it,' Luke said. 'But Parker is in a choir. The kid is a singer.'

# FORTY-SEVEN

Caitlin asked Luke, Hana and Nicolson if she could meet with Grace's family. The trio of detectives decided to wait until the media frenzy had died down a bit and the journalists who had set up camp outside of the Feist's home once again, had finally left.

Philippa Nicolson drove up from her home in Sussex to take Caitlin over to the Feists and it was an emotional reunion for all of them. While the Feist family would never have Grace back, they had, in some small way, been reconnected to Grace and to her life through someone who had been almost a sister to their daughter.

'Any chance you're going to come out of retirement now, Philippa?' Luke asked her.

'Zero chance, Wiley,' she said when she stopped by the seventh floor of Scotland Yard to say a final goodbye before heading back to her home, her garden, and her husband.

'It was good to meet you,' Hana said. 'We never got to finish our drink.'

'No,' Nicolson replied. 'But I have the feeling that we may one day. You know where I am.'

Hana nodded, finding herself surprised that she wished Nicolson was sticking around.

The Serious Crime Unit had felt quiet over the past six weeks after Poppy Travis was found and returned to her grateful family. The Incident Room had been dismantled and Rowdy had actually taken a week's holiday.

Luke and Hana had a mountain of paperwork to catch up on and O'Donnell had once again reminded them that the harassment case they had dropped in order to work on Grace Feist's murder, still needed to be completed.

Hana had offered to come by Luke's place on Arlington Square later that evening. The suggestion was supposed to be a gentle message for her partner — that she was okay and they could resume their hunt for Sadie's killer.

She hadn't told Luke about her conversation over breakfast with Henry MacAskill, and part of her wanted to do her own digging first. What did he mean and what was he trying to tell her?

'Sure,' Luke said, understanding completely what Hana was saying to him. He had a new theory about what had happened to his wife, and the only person he trusted to tell was Hana. Maybe one day he would tell his therapist, but not yet. For now, Luke was still sleeping soundly through the night, but if he was right, all of that was about to change.

# IF YOU ENJOYED THE QUIET AND THE DEAD...

Please consider leaving a rating or a review on Amazon, it really helps new readers discover DCI Luke Wiley and the team.

DCI Luke Wiley returns in

**The Killing Pages**

# About the Author

JAYE BAILEY is a writer living in London. She is a big fan of true crime and detective fiction and the characters of Luke, Sadie and Hana have been in her head for a long time. Jaye finally decided to put pen to paper and begin the DCI Luke Wiley series.

When she's not writing, Jaye loves to travel. When at home, her house seems to be the destination house of choice for all the neighbourhood cats and, in her humble opinion, she makes the best spaghetti bolognese on the planet. (Yes, she will send you the recipe.)

Find out more at: jayebaileybooks.com

# TWO
# YARDS

Printed in Great Britain
by Amazon